The Devil
and his
Boy

ANTHONY HOROWITZ

WALKER BOOKS
AND SUBSIDIARIES
LONDON · BOSTON · SYDNEY · AUCKLAND

First published 1998 by Walker Books Ltd
87 Vauxhall Walk, London SE11 5HJ

This edition published 2004

2 4 6 8 10 9 7 5 3

Text © 1998 Anthony Horowitz
Cover illustration © 2004 David Frankland

The right of Anthony Horowitz to be identified as author
of this work has been asserted by him in accordance
with the Copyright, Designs and Patents Act 1988

This book has been typeset in Sabon

Printed in Great Britain by Cox & Wyman Ltd, Reading, Berkshire

British Library Cataloguing in Publication Data:
a catalogue record for this book
is available from the British Library

ISBN 1-84428-606-1

www.walkerbooks.co.uk

THE DEVIL AND HIS BOY

Anthony Horowitz is a popular and prolific children's writer, whose books have been translated into over twenty four languages. They include *Stormbreaker*, *Point Blanc*, *Skeleton Key*, the No.1 bestseller *Eagle Strike* and *Scorpia* which chronicle the adventures of reluctant teenage MI6 spy, Alex Rider. Amongst his other titles are *Groosham Grange* and its sequel, *Return to Groosham Grange*; *Granny*; *The Switch*; and the Diamond Brothers Trilogy – *The Falcon's Malteser* (which has been filmed with the title *Just Ask for Diamond*) followed by *South by South East* (which was dramatized in six parts on TV) and *Public Enemy Number Two* – to which three other short novels: *I Know What You Did Last Wednesday*, *The French Confection* and *The Blurred Man* have been added. Anthony also writes extensively for TV and film, with credits including *Murder in Mind*; *Foyle's War*; *Midsomer Murders*; *Poirot*; *Murder Most Horrid* and the block-buster Hollywood movie, *The Gathering*, starring Christina Ricci. Anthony is married to the television producer, Jill Green, and lives in north London with his two children, Nicholas and Cassian, and their dog, Lucky.

CONTENTS

THE STONE OF VISION

It was just before midnight when Queen Elizabeth slipped out of bed and went in search of her magician.

Although she had allowed her Maids of Honour to lead her into the bedroom and help her undress more than an hour before, she hadn't even tried to sleep. Part of the trouble, of course, was being Queen of England. She could still feel the crown on her head even when she wasn't wearing it ... there was so much to think about, so much to do. But the real problem was her bed. It was a huge, four-postered thing with no fewer than five quilts. The first was silk, the next velvet, then there was a gold one and a silver one and finally, on top, a quilt embroidered with a rather gloomy picture of the Sermon on the Mount. The quilts had been given to her by the Spanish ambassador, the French ambassador, the

Dutch ambassador, the German ambassador and the Archbishop of Canterbury and she had to use them all in case she gave offence to any one of them. The result was that even on the coldest winter nights she was always much too hot.

For a moment she stood in the middle of the room and glanced out of the window. There was a full moon that night which pleased the Queen. She knew that the magician would like it. Somehow his spells always worked better when there was a moon and this one seemed huge, a perfect white circle hanging in the darkness. Her eyes travelled down and she saw the Thames, ash white as it twisted through the city of London. Everything was silent. The Queen nodded. This was the right time.

She crossed the room to a tapestry which covered an entire wall. The tapestry showed a lion being hunted and, when she was young, the snarling face with its awful eyes had given her nightmares. But she was an elderly woman now. Sixty years old. And being Queen was often nightmare enough.

The tapestry was suspended from a rail and she pulled it aside to reveal a bare brick wall with no visible door or window. At the far end, over a bookshelf, there was a metal hook and without hesitating the Queen went over to it and turned it. There was a click and a whole section of the wall swung inwards on a hidden hinge to reveal a jagged opening and a spiral staircase leading down. Grey cobwebs hung in the air. A fat black spider, frightened by the light from the bedroom, tumbled down the brickwork and then scuttled along the floor, disappearing into the shadows.

The Queen lifted a candle from her room and started forward. After the warmth of the bedroom the stairs were very cold. A draft twisted round her ankles and slithered up her legs. The candle in her hand flickered and her shadow seemed to jump away, tugging at her as if it could pull her back upstairs. For a moment she wondered if this was a good idea. She could still turn back, go to bed and forget all about it. The Queen was afraid. But a single question had tormented her for more than forty years. She had to know the answer. She had to know it now.

She continued down. A moth, attracted by the light, flew into her face. Its feathery wings brushed against her lips and she gasped out loud. Her hand banged against the wall and she almost dropped the candle. She stopped for a minute, catching her breath, then, gripping the candle more tightly, she followed the stairs to their end, passing through an archway and along a corridor where the ceiling curved low over her head as if groaning under the weight of the great palace a hundred metres above.

She had reached a door made of thick planks of wood bound together with iron and so low that she had to bend to open it. It reminded her of the door of one of her own dungeons. Her hand found a silver ring and she turned it, the metal cold against her skin. On the other side, a warm yellow glow and the faint smell of rosemary welcomed her into a small, circular chamber. The door swung shut behind her as she went in.

"Good evening, Queen."

"You were expecting me, Wizard?"

"Oh yes. I knew you were going to come and visit me before you had decided it yourself. Sit down..."

Nobody else would have dared to talk to Queen Elizabeth in this way. For a start she should have been called "Your Royal Highness" or "Your Majesty". And nobody ever told her what to do – not even so much as to sit down. But the person seated in the high wooden-backed chair was no ordinary man.

Dr John Dee was sixty-six years old but looked much older, having a white moustache and a white beard that came to a point about halfway down his chest. He wore a long black robe and a black cap that could have been painted on to his head. His eyes were brown – a strange, watery brown, the colour of melted chocolate. There was a grey cat, half asleep, on his lap and he occasionally stroked it with a long, elegant finger. Dr Dee spoke with a Welsh accent. So, rather more remarkably, did the cat.

"So you know why I am here," the Queen said.

"Of course I do."

"Do you know everything, Wizard?"

Dr Dee shook his head. "I know many things, Queen. And my stone of vision tells me more. But only God knows everything and I am just a man."

"Can you tell me when I am going to die?" the Queen asked.

The magician hesitated. His eyes narrowed and he seemed unsure what to say. Then the cat arched its back, stretched its legs and suddenly opened its quite brilliant emerald eyes. "You'll die," the cat said, "when you stop breathing."

There was a silence in the room. For a long minute the Queen gazed at the cat. Then she smiled. "It's a good answer," she said.

"But that isn't the question you came to ask," Dee muttered.

"No." Suddenly the Queen was nervous. Her fingers closed on a gold locket she was wearing round her neck. She had taken all her other jewellery off for bed. But this locket never left her. It was part of her. "I have to know about him," she said.

"Why now?"

"Because I can't wait any longer. I think of him all the time, Wizard. I know I can never see him but I still wonder about him – whether he is dead or alive."

Dr Dee stroked the cat. "I can tell you what you want to know," he said. "But I have to warn you now, Queen. It might be better not to ask. Magic has a nasty way of changing things. You cast a spell, you ask for secret knowledge and before you know what you've done you've opened a barrel of worms ... or something worse than worms if you're unlucky."

"I still have to know," the Queen insisted. "Enough of this, Wizard. You've known me long enough to know when my mind is made up. Do your magic. Tell me what you see."

"She's making a mistake!" the cat murmured.

"Hush!" Dr Dee stroked the cat, then lifted it up and set it to one side.

There was a low table between Dr Dee and the Queen, a number of objects scattered across the top. These were the tools of the magician's trade. There were three or four old books, so old that the words seemed to be sinking into the thick, yellowy pages. There were two candles and a tapering wand. Between them lay what looked like an ordinary piece of silvery-grey stone, about the size of a dinner plate. Dr Dee picked it up and

12

cradled it in his hands.

"I will need something of his," Dee said in a low voice.

Once again the Queen's fingers reached for the locket round her neck but this time she took it and drew it over her head. Nestling it in the palm of one hand, she opened it with the other. Inside the locket was the miniature portrait of a man and opposite it, a lock of light brown hair. The Queen gazed at the hair for what seemed like an eternity, then she let it fall on to the table. "It's all I have," she said.

"You're prepared to lose it?"

There was a flicker of anger in the Queen's eyes. "Do what you have to," she said.

Dr Dee picked up the hair and laid it on the stone. His hands were still cupped round it but now he moved them away a little, his eyes fixed on the stone as if he were trying to look through it. The Queen leaned forward and as she did so, the lock of hair moved. She thought that it had been caught in a draught but then she realized that the stone had become hot and that it was the heat that was causing the effect. The air above the stone was shimmering. The colour of the stone was changing: from grey to white and then to metallic silver.

"No...!" The word escaped the Queen's lips as a whisper. The lock of hair had burst into flame. Now the flickering pieces rose into the air, twisted and disappeared. The surface of

13

the stone was no longer rough or remotely stony. It had become a mirror but as Dr Dee looked into it, it did not show his reflection.

"His name was Robert." The magician's eyes were focused far away and the Queen knew that he was seeing things outside the room, outside and far away.

"Yes. Robert..." Even uttering his name was a knife-wound. She had never done it before. "Tell me, Wizard. Is he alive?"

A long silence. And then...

"No, Queen. He is dead."

The Queen fell back in her chair, covering her eyes with her hands. Somehow she had always expected it but like all bad news it had lost none of its power to hurt. But Dr Dee was still gazing into the mirror that had been a stone and there was a look of puzzlement on his face.

"What is it?" the Queen demanded.

"I don't know..." And then, as if a cloud had parted and the sun had broken through, the magician looked up. "He had a son," he said.

"What?"

"Robert is dead but his son is still alive."

The Queen gripped the sides of her chair. "Where is he? What is he called? What do you know about him?"

"He's far from here. I can't see his name." The stone was getting hotter and hotter. The very air inside the chamber was beginning to burn.

"Try! You must try!"

"No. All I can see is a castle and a pig. It's very difficult..." Dr Dee waved a hand over the stone, clearing the smoke. "The pig is outside the castle and over the boy."

"He's still a boy? How old is he?"

"Twelve. The castle..." Dr Dee frowned. "They're building chimneys on the castle. Strange-looking chimneys. I can see the boy limping past the castle and he's looking at the chimneys and..."

"Why is he limping?"

"Because of the pig..."

"Why must your answers be so mysterious, Wizard? Where is the boy? If you can't tell me his name, at least tell me where he is!"

But before Dr Dee could reply, there was a sudden crackle as if something were short-circuiting. At the same time, the mirror shattered, a thousand cracks exploding across its surface. Then the cracks faded and a second later the stone was exactly as it had been, lying flat and ordinary on the table.

"That's all I can tell you, Queen." Dr Dee picked up the stone. It was quite cool to touch. "But you have spies and men of intelligence. It should be enough."

"A castle, strange chimneys and a pig. It's another of your wretched riddles, Wizard. Where do I even start?"

"Framlingham!" The cat – which had been

quite forgotten during all this – leapt on to Dr Dee's lap. "They're building chimneys on Framlingham Castle."

"How do you know?" the Queen asked.

The cat shrugged. "A little bird told me," it remarked. "And then I ate the little bird."

"Framlingham ... in Suffolk." The Queen got to her feet. "Only four or five days from here. You've done well, Wizard. You have my thanks and will have much more!"

The Queen left, climbing back up the secret staircase to her bedroom. She was still awake when the sun rose above the thatched roofs and wooden houses of London and the first horses stumbled along the rough, pitted tracks that were the city's roads. The year was 1593. The Queen, of course, was Elizabeth I. And she was already planning the course of events that would change one boy's life for ever and with it the entire history of the country she ruled.

THE PIG'S HEAD

It was raining in Framlingham; a cold, grey, December rain that dripped and trickled into every corner and wiped away the colour of everything it touched. The streets were so full of puddles that there were more puddles than street, with only a few patches of brown mud here and there to remind you that the place had once been built on dry land. The two moats surrounding Framlingham Castle were full to overflowing. The town gardens and bowling green had disappeared.

The inn stood just outside the town, next to a large swamp. It was a squat, dark, evil-smelling place with rotting timbers and mouldy walls. It had few windows – glass was too expensive – but the noise of singing and the smell of roasting meat seeped through the thatched roof and chimney. An inn sign swung in the wind. The sign showed the head of a pig, severed from its body, for that was the inn's name.

THE PIG'S HEAD, FRAMLINGHAM
PROPRIETORS: SEBASTIAN & HENRIETTA
SLOPE

At about five o'clock in the afternoon a young boy came out of the inn carrying a bucket. Despite the weather, he was wearing only the lightest of clothes: a shirt open at the neck, a waistcoat that was too short for him, a pair of trousers that flapped around his ankles. He had neither shoes nor socks. His bare feet splashed in the mud as he went to draw water from the well.

The boy was about twelve or thirteen years old. Nobody knew or cared when exactly he had been born. He had long, reddish-brown hair, pale skin and bright, intelligent blue eyes. He was painfully thin – his rags seemed to hang off his shoulders without actually touching his body and there was a bruise on the side of his cheek, the size of a man's fist. He lowered the bucket into the well, gripping the handle that groaned rustily as it turned; his fingers were unusually long and slender. The boy's name was Thomas Falconer. That, at least, would be the name they'd carve on his gravestone when starvation or the plague carried him away. For now they simply called him Tom.

He was about to lift the bucket out of the well when a sound made him turn. A man had appeared, a traveller on horseback, his body lost in the folds of a dark cloak and his face hidden by his hat. The horse was a great black stallion with a white blaze on its chest. Steam snorted from its nostrils as it jerked forward, its hooves striking angrily in the mud. It came to a halt and the rider swung himself effortlessly down. Mud had splattered his leather boots and the bottom of his cloak. He had evidently been riding for some time.

"Boy!" The man called out.

Forgetting the bucket, Tom ran to obey. "Yes, sir?"

"Take the horse to the stable. See that he's watered and fed. If any harm comes to him, you'll answer for it."

The man dragged his luggage from behind his saddle and handed the reins to Tom. He was about to turn away but suddenly he stopped and for a moment Tom found himself being examined by two narrow, grey eyes in a dark, weathered face.

"What's your name, boy?" the man demanded.

"Tom, sir." Tom was surprised. People seldom took any notice of him.

"How long have you worked here, Tom?"

"All my life, sir. Ever since I was able to work."

19

The rider stared at Tom as if trying to read something in his face. "Your parents own this place?" he asked.

Tom shook his head. "My parents are dead," he said.

"Who were they? Do you know?"

It was one question too many. Travellers often passed through Framlingham on their way to the ports at Harwich and Ipswich, but they came as strangers and that was how they left. It was the unwritten law. In an uncertain world, it could be dangerous to give too much information about yourself.

Tom's lips clamped shut. The man seemed to understand. "Look after the horse, Tom," he said and walked into the inn.

The inn was crowded, the fire a distant red glimmer behind so many huddled bodies. Thick smoke coiled upwards from the hearth, from the tallow candles on the mantle and from pipes clenched in the teeth of men, and women too. Two more boys – older and better fed than Tom – were bustling in and out of the kitchen carrying wooden trenchers of meat and bread, somehow forcing their way through the great tangle to find the tables beyond. Someone somewhere was playing a fiddle but the sound was almost drowned out by the shouting, arguing, laughing and drunken singing of the guests.

The landlord noticed the new arrival the

moment the door opened but then he had the sort of eyes that noticed everything. This was Sebastian Slope. He was a small, nervous man who had never quite recovered from the pox which had ravaged his skin and eaten away part of his nose. He had tried to grow a beard and moustache to hide the damage but unfortunately the hair – as well as being bright orange – was thin and uneven, sprouting in one part of his face but not in another with the result that he looked as if he had been horribly injured – perhaps by a musket at close range.

Rubbing his pale, white hands together he approached the new arrival who was standing there waiting, water dripping from his cloak.

"Good evening, my lord. Welcome. Welcome to the Pig's Head." Slope's teeth had long ago rotted away – all but a couple of them – and he now found it easier to speak through what was left of his nose. His voice was thin and high-pitched. If a rat could talk it would probably sound much the same. "What can I do for you, my lord? A pint of the finest ale? A delicious supper? A nice leg of mutton? Or perhaps the speciality of the house. A potato! Have you ever tried a potato, my lord? It is quite new and the most remarkable thing…"

"I need a room for the night," the traveller interrupted.

"Of course. Of course. We can provide you with the best linen sheets. And only six of our guests have slept on them since they were last washed…"

"I'll have a bed with clean sheets. And I'll eat some lamb. Yes. And a rabbit too. Mushrooms. Some cheese. And beer not ale."

"Beer. Yes. Yes. Will you eat in your chamber, my lord, or at the common table? It'll be sixpence downstairs and eightpence up, but if you have it up perhaps we could arrange for one of our kitchen maids to keep you company…?"

"I'll eat down here."

"You do us all a privilege, my lord." Slope twisted a smile on to his lips but at the same time a strange gleam had come into his eyes so that he looked both servile and sinister at the same time. "Have you come far, my lord?"

"From London," the stranger replied.

"And returning soon?"

"Tomorrow."

This was the information that the innkeeper had been angling for. He swallowed once, his adam's apple performing a somersault in his scrawny throat. "Henrietta!" he called out. "Henny!"

A moment later a tiny woman with grey, straggly hair hurried out of the smoke. This was Henrietta Slope and although to look at she could have been Sebastian's grandmother, she was in fact his wife. She too had caught the pox – in seventeen years' marriage it was the

22

only thing her husband had given her. The disease had attacked her lips which had shrivelled away so that when she smiled she was forced to use her teeth.

"We have a guest," Sebastian said.

"A guest! How lovely! And a gentleman!" Henrietta curtsied twice. "Have you ordered food, my lord? The food here is a delight. We've only had nine cases of food poisoning since our new cook started!"

"I've ordered," the traveller muttered.

"He has indeed," Sebastian agreed. "Lamb. Mushrooms. Cheese. And rabbit…"

"Rabbit?" Henrietta grinned liplessly. "Fresh today. It couldn't be fresher. In fact, I strangled it myself."

"Thank you." The traveller seemed to be in a hurry to get away from this odd couple but suddenly he leaned across the bar and drew them closer to him. "I was talking just now to that boy outside…" he began.

"Tom?" Sebastian's face darkened. "If he offended your lordship, I'll throw him down the well."

"That boy's useless!" Henrietta shrieked. "He's worse than useless. He's a drip. He's a damp patch. A dead worm!"

"He hasn't offended me," the traveller interrupted. "I'm merely interested in him. Where did you find him?"

Sebastian glanced at his wife then leered at

the new guest. "Are you interested in buying him?" he asked.

"We might sell him," Henrietta simpered. "Although of course we'd miss him. He works very well for us. A very hard worker. Very fit..." She seemed to have completely forgotten what she had been saying only a few moments before.

"Where did you find him?"

"He was an orphan." Henrietta's eyes filled with tears. "I have two sons of my own, sir. I took him in out of the goodness of my heart." She tapped her chest which seemed too thin and hollow to contain any heart at all. "We look after him in return for a few light tasks about the house..."

"What of his parents?" the traveller asked, becoming more interested by the second.

"They worked up at the castle," Sebastian replied. "The father fell off a horse and broke his neck. The mother died giving birth to him. He came into the world with nothing and if it weren't for Mrs S and me, nothing is all he'd have now."

The traveller's eyes narrowed and for a moment he said nothing. He was obviously deep in thought. But then he shook his head and straightened up. "Send me my food as soon as possible," he said and went and sat at the nearest table.

Sebastian Slope watched the man as he took

his place, then slipped through a door and into the kitchen. Here there was a second, huge fire with a rather angry-looking pig on a spit being turned by a fat, sweating cook with dirty hands and a runny nose. Henrietta had followed her husband in and now he drew her to one side, standing over a huge cauldron of soup that was slowly congealing.

"What do you think, my precious?" he asked.

"Rich," Henrietta murmured. "Definitely rich."

"That's what I thought." Sebastian tried to pick his nose, remembered it wasn't there and bit his nail absent-mindedly instead. "Did you notice the cloak – lined with velvet, my jewel? And the boots…"

Henrietta nodded. "I think this is one for Ratsey," she muttered.

"Yes," Sebastian said. "Ratsey will like this one. You'd better call the boy."

But at that very moment the outer door opened and Tom came back into the kitchen. It had begun to rain more heavily and water dripped out of his hair, running down the side of his neck. He was carrying the bucket, full now and heavy.

"Where have you been?" Sebastian swung a lazy arm and slapped the back of his hand across Tom's head.

"Lazing again, I'll be bound!" Henrietta did

the same, only harder.

"I'm sorry!" Tom cried out. "A gentleman came. He told me to see to his horse."

"Yes." Sebastian leaned closer. Tom cowered away but the landlord was smiling. "What sort of a horse does he ride?"

"A stallion. Black with a white mark."

"Valuable?"

Tom hesitated. He knew what was about to happen and thought about lying but it was no good. The Slopes would know. They always did. "Yes," he said.

Sebastian grabbed him by the collar and drew him so close that his lips almost touched the boy's ear. "You're to go into the wood," he whispered. "Find Ratsey. Tell him we have a mark. The London road. Tomorrow…"

"But it's dark. It's raining…"

"Are you arguing with me?" Sebastian hadn't raised his voice but his grip had tightened and his eyes, dark to begin with, had gone almost black.

"No."

"Then be off with you. To the burnt oak. And if he isn't there, wait for him to come."

Tom ran out, slamming the door behind him. Sebastian and Henrietta Slope watched him go.

"You're too good to that child," Henrietta sighed.

"I'm too soft-hearted, I know it," Sebastian agreed.

"I wonder why our guest was so interested in him?" Henrietta scratched her head and sighed as a lump of hair fell into the soup. Her disease was definitely getting worse.

Sebastian considered for a moment. "I don't suppose we'll ever know," he replied.

Husband and wife kissed each other, grey lipless teeth on to grey pock-marked flesh. Then they left the kitchen and went back into the inn.

GAMALIEL RATSEY

After he had left the Pig's Head, Tom climbed up the hill and back into the town centre. It had stopped raining and the clouds had parted enough to allow a slice of moonlight to cut through. Tom was grateful for it. Without the moon he would have had to make the journey in almost pitch blackness for the only other light came from the candles burning behind the windows of the houses and – with the high price of wax – there were few enough of them.

He passed through the market square, skirting an old, crooked building that stood in the middle. This was called the Market Cross and Tom knew that there was a schoolroom on the upper floor. Not that he had ever been inside it. He had never been to school, not even for a day. He had never learned to read or write anything more than the three letters of his own name.

Tom was an orphan who had never known his parents. He was beaten and bullied every day. He was half starved and owned nothing more than the rags he was wearing. And yet despite all this he wouldn't have described himself as unhappy. For a start he had never once been outside Framlingham so he had nothing with which to compare his own life. At the same time, he had listened to travellers staying at the inn and knew that there were poor people and hungry people all over England – so why should things be any different for him? At least he had a roof over his head – even if it was only a stable roof which leaked in the rain. He had plenty of scraps and left-overs to eat. The Slopes might beat him but so far they hadn't broken anything. All in all, things could be worse.

Ahead of him, Framlingham Castle loomed up, its walls dark and ancient against the night sky. Tom had heard about the great banquets and tournaments that had taken place there years ago. But that was all in the past. Now the castle was crumbling. Cracks had appeared in the brickwork and weeds had quickly sprouted in the cracks. The ridiculous, twisting chimneys which had been added to the battlements were just its final humiliation.

Tom hurried round it, keeping the town ditch on his left. The town seemed to end very suddenly. The road became a track. The track grew more and more uneven. And then he was walking across a bumpy field with a black, skeletal forest springing up ahead.

Most of the trees had lost their leaves. The forest in winter was a cold, forbidding place. As Tom continued, branches twisted and interlocked above his head while roots formed tangled knots beneath him. The glistening tree trunks were like huge bars. With every step he took he felt himself being swallowed up by a vast, living cage.

Somewhere, far away, an animal howled in the darkness. One of the dogs from the village? Or something worse? Tom knew that it was unlikely that wolves would come so far south at this time of year – but even so he found himself quickening his pace.

He had been this way many times and soon found what he was looking for. A tree shaped like a Y, a rough slope covered in white pebbles, a circular clearing and there on the far side, an old oak tree that had been hit by lightning, split in half and burned coal black. This was the burnt oak that Sebastian Slope had referred to. This was where Ratsey would be found.

Ratsey.

Tom realized that he was shivering and wondered if it was entirely due to the cold. He drew two fingers into his mouth and whistled a high-pitched note, then a lower one. It was a signal he had used often although he still had no idea how Ratsey heard it, where he came from, how he knew when someone was about to arrive. The sound should have echoed through the trees but on this damp, dreary night the whistle sounded very small. Tom lifted his fingers again, then hesitated as a second terrible howl ripped through the dark sky. It *was* a wolf. It couldn't be anything else.

"Tom, Tom, the piper's son…"

The voice was hushed, singing the words with a soft laugh. Tom turned round and almost cried out. A moment ago there had been no one there but now there was a man, dressed in a long leather coat with a sword at his waist. At least, he was man up to the neck. He had the head of some sort of horrible monster with bloodshot eyes that bulged out of their sockets, yellow teeth as thick as piano keys, swollen cheeks like over-ripe melons and a chin that curved round until it almost touched his nose.

The man finished his song. "Tom, Tom, the piper's son. Will he stay or will he run?"

Tom relaxed, recognizing the voice. "Ratsey!" he exclaimed.

"Did I scare you, Tom?"

"No…"

"A shame. I meant to."

Ratsey laughed, then reached up and grabbed hold of his chin. He pulled and his entire face came away – it was nothing more than an elaborate mask. The face underneath it was an unusually handsome one with black hair sweeping over the forehead and almost touching the man's shoulders. His eyes, alight with humour, were pale blue and the more he smiled, the brighter they seemed to shine. But for his sword, his leather coat (patched in so many places that there must have been very little of the original coat left) and his mud-spattered boots, you might have taken him for a priest or a choirboy. But then, if you had looked deeper into those eyes, you might have noticed how very black his pupils were and if at that moment he were to stop smiling you would realize that this was a man who would never come near a church – unless it was to burn it down.

"What do you think of the new mask?" he demanded. He held it up so that its pointed nose almost touched his own.

"It's horrible," Tom replied.

"Thank you." He set the mask down. "And now, I wonder what brings you out on this wet and wicked night?"

Tom swallowed. "There's a man," he said. "A traveller."

"Is he rich?"

"Master Slope says he might be."

"Might be?" Ratsey laughed and pulled a metal bottle from somewhere inside his coat.

He unscrewed the lid, raised it to his lips and swallowed. "Tell me what you think, Tom-Tom! Is he rich?"

"I don't know, Ratsey."

Ratsey considered this statement for a moment. He lowered the bottle and smacked his lips. He sighed. He sucked his teeth. And then, before Tom could move, he lashed out, grabbing hold of the boy's ear and dragging him towards him with such force that Tom cried out with pain.

"I asked you a question," he said in a reasonable tone of voice. "When I ask a question I expect an answer. That's the whole point."

"He's rich!" Tom shouted. He could feel his ear coming away from his head. "He's got a good horse. Black, with white markings. His clothes are smart. He has money."

"Which way is he coming?"

"The London road!"

"Excellent!" Ratsey let go and Tom reeled back, clutching his ear. Ratsey gazed at him apologetically, then handed him the bottle. "Here you go, old chap," he said. "Have a swig of that. It'll take away some of the cold."

Tom hesitated but Ratsey gestured and he raised the bottle to his lips. It contained some sort of brandy. "In a strange way, you remind me of me when I was young," Ratsey said. "Not of course that I was as scrawny and ragged as you. As a matter of fact, my father was a duke." He winked. "Strange to think that when I was your age I ate off gold plates and had servants to do everything for me."

"So what happened, Ratsey?"

Ratsey smiled. "I got bored and I ran away. I went to war." He reached out, took the bottle and drank. For a long moment he stared into the distance and Tom could see the moon reflected in his eyes. "Captain Ratsey – that was me. I fought for the Queen in Ireland. Good old Queeny! I saw her once, you know, Tom-Tom. She was as close to me as that tree over there." He nodded at the oak. "Glorious days! But then times got hard. No money. No food. No fun..." He jerked his head to one side as if shaking off the memory and suddenly he was business-like again. "Tell Slope that I'll be waiting," he said.

"Yes, Ratsey."

Ratsey gestured with his head and Tom set off at once, scrabbling across the clearing and back up the slope. When he reached the top, he stopped and turned round. But the clearing was already empty. Ratsey had vanished as quickly and quietly as he had appeared and the burnt oak stood solitary, dead in the pale glow of the moon.

It was still dark when Tom opened his eyes the following morning. In the summer months he would be woken by the sun breaking through the cracks in the walls of the stable where he slept but in the winter it was always the cold that did it.

As he set to work, Tom thought about Ratsey and about the traveller who would be leaving for London that day. He knew what was going to happen. The same thing had been going on for as long as he could remember. But there was nothing he could do about it. It was no business of his.

Tom had just finished cleaning out the hearth – the ashes thick with fat and grease – when he became aware of voices in the main room. The first, high-pitched in anger and indignation, he knew at once. It was Sebastian Slope.

"You can't take him!" he was saying. "I won't let you!"

"You'll hang if you try to stop me."

A moment later the door opened and the traveller stormed in, already dressed in his cloak and with his sword buckled at his waist. Sebastian Slope was right behind him. The innkeeper had obviously got up in a hurry. He was wearing a dirty vest, hanging outside his trousers. His eyes were bleary and his orange hair was even more dishevelled than usual.

The traveller ignored him. His attention was fixed on Tom, kneeling by the hearth. "Tom," he said, "do you have any possessions? Anything you call your own?"

"No, sir." Tom was too dazed to understand what was happening.

"Then you have nothing to pack. Come with me. We're leaving now."

"But … my lord!" Slope's blustering hadn't worked so now he began to whine. "My wife and I … where would we be without the boy? We've treated him like a son…"

"You've treated him like a slave and believe me, you will hear more of it."

"You don't want him, my lord!" Slope was actually crying but – rather repulsively – the tears were coming out of what was left of his nose. "He's no good to you. He's a sneak. He's a sniveller. If it wasn't for Mrs S and me he'd have been hanged years ago."

"Tell me, boy…" he said – the traveller was standing firmly between Tom and the innkeeper – "do you want to stay with this man and his wife?"

Tom wasn't sure what to say. He certainly had no love for either of the Slopes, but to leave…? To step outside the small world of Framlingham? It was something he had never even for a minute considered.

"He wants to stay!" Sebastian Slope exclaimed. "He loves Mrs S and me. Like we was his own parents."

"No!" Tom was amazed to find himself saying it. "I don't want to stay."

"Then let's go."

With his back turned to him, the traveller didn't see the landlord snatch up a knife that had been lying on a table. Tom opened his mouth to call out a warning – but the traveller had no need of it. He must have heard something, for in less than a second his sword was out of its sheath. He spun round and slashed down twice. The first stroke gashed Slope's arm, drawing a thin line of blood. The second sliced across his stomach and for a horrible moment Tom was sure it had killed him. But the blade had only cut through the waistband of his trousers. As Sebastian Slope howled in pain, they slid down to his ankles, exposing a pair of knees like over-sized conkers.

"This way, Tom."

Not sure if he was awake or asleep, Tom followed the traveller out into the yard and watched as he saddled and made ready his horse. It didn't take him very long. As he led the animal out of the stable, he smiled at Tom for the first time. "You've never ridden a horse," he said.

"No, sir."

"It's not difficult. You'll sit behind me and hold on to me. You'll soon get used to it."

"Where are you taking me, sir?"

"To London."

London!

London was a four-day ride away but for Tom it could have been on the other side of the planet ... on the other side of the moon even. London was a city, he knew, with a tower and a river and a cathedral so great that the church at Framlingham could fit inside it. He had heard it said that crowds of people lived there; not just dozens of people but hundreds, maybe even a thousand.

He tried to speak but couldn't find the words. In silence, he allowed the traveller to help him on to the horse and clung to the saddle, hardly daring to move. He was much higher than he had imagined and he was grateful when the traveller climbed up and sat before him.

"Say goodbye to it, Tom," the man said. "You're starting a new life."

But before they could move, there was a screech and Henrietta Slope emerged from the inn. Her husband was right behind her, holding up his trousers with his good hand.

"What are you doing?" she squealed. "You've no right! I'll have the law on to you."

"I am the law," the traveller replied. "And you have every reason to fear me. But although you don't deserve it, I'll play fair with you." He threw a handful of coins into the mud. "This is for my room and board. Now be silent and let us pass."

The traveller kicked with his feet and the horse trotted forward. At the same time, Henrietta threw herself in front of it. Tom wasn't sure what happened next. The horse reared up and he clung on for dear life. Henrietta fell back, losing her balance. With a great scream, she crashed to the ground, slap into the middle of a pile of soft and steaming horse manure. Sebastian tried to help her but, with his trousers in a knot, he was too slow.

The horse had left the courtyard. Tom and the traveller were gone. Henrietta Slope took her husband's hand and allowed him to pull her to her feet. She gazed down the road at the horse with its two figures already vanishing into the distance. "Are you all right?" Sebastian asked.

Henrietta wiped a hand across the back of her leg. "I stink!" she exclaimed.

"I know, my dear," Sebastian agreed. "But don't worry. The horse manure will hide it." He held up his hand, blood trickling between his fingers. "He cut me!" he complained.

Henrietta looked at the blood, then back at the road. "It's nothing compared to what Ratsey will do to him," she muttered.

"Ratsey…!" Sebastian had forgotten but now an ugly light came into his eyes. He tore a piece off the bottom of his vest and wrapped it round his hand. "You think he'll find him?"

"He'll find him. Ratsey never misses." Henrietta's cheeks twitched as she tried to draw lips that weren't there into a triumphant smile. "We'll have the boy back – aye and that fine horse with him. And as for our brave traveller…"

"Dead meat, Mrs S."

"Dead and buried, my beloved."

And laughing softly to themselves, the innkeeper and his wife turned and began to scavenge for the coins in the mud where they'd been thrown.

THE AMBUSH

He was leaving Framlingham!

As he watched the last traces of the village disappear behind him, Tom still couldn't believe it was happening. He had been born in Framlingham. He had lived his whole life there. And he'd always assumed he would die there – probably quite soon. And not only was he leaving ... he was on a horse! The Slopes could never have afforded a horse like this, even with all the money they had stolen. The only animal they'd ever owned had been a dog and that had gone mad when they forgot to feed it.

It was the man who broke the silence.

"Tom," he said, "do you have a second name?"

"My father's name was Falconer, sir," Tom replied. "At least, that was what they put on his gravestone. But I've only ever been Tom."

"And my name is Hawkins," the traveller said. "Sir William Hawkins." He smiled. "A hawk and a falcon. We make a good pair."

Hawkins pulled on the reins and the horse stopped. He twisted in the saddle and gazed at the boy behind him. His eyes narrowed. He reached out and brushed the hair out of Tom's eyes, his fingers stroking the boy's forehead. "It is most wonderful," he muttered. "You remind me of someone. I knew it the moment I first set eyes on you. But who? There's the mystery. Who indeed?"

He turned round and the horse moved off again.

"Are we really going to London?" Tom asked.

"We are."

"But why? What do you want with me?"

"It's not for me to answer your questions, Tom," Hawkins replied. "I was told to find you and that's what I've done. But for the rest of it … you'll have to wait until we arrive."

Until we arrive.

But would they?

Ever since they had set out another fear had been stirring in Tom's mind. Gamaliel Ratsey was somewhere out there. Maybe he was watching them even now. Tom glanced around him. On one side there were fields, cut into narrow strips with rough trenches in between. On the other, trees were already beginning to thicken into a wood which would soon surround them. Hawkins had spoken of the road to London, but of course there was no real road. They were following a track that was so faint it was barely a track at all. There was nobody else in sight.

"Why are we going this way?" Tom asked.

"It's the way I came," Hawkins replied.

"Is this the only way to London?"

"It's the fastest way. Why, Tom? What's the matter?"

Tom wasn't sure how to answer. Part of him wanted to tell Hawkins all about Ratsey and to plead with him to go another way. But at the same time he was too afraid to speak. It was he, after all, who had informed Ratsey about the traveller only the night before – as he had done many times in the past. Tom had never been a willing part of it but even so he knew that if Ratsey were discovered, he would hang with him.

The forest grew thicker, the silence more profound. Above them, a black crow launched itself out of a tree with a sudden scream. Tom could bear it no more.

"Please, Mr Hawkins!" he exclaimed. "You have to go another way. You're in danger..."

But it was already too late.

Ahead of them, a figure suddenly stepped out, something long and metallic in its hand. The horse reared and tried to find a way round. But there were thick briars on either

43

side. There was no other way.

Gamaliel Ratsey was wearing another, even more disgusting mask. This one showed the head of a fish, but a fish that was already dead and rotting. Its eyes were white and sightless. Its lips were disfigured as if torn by the fisherman's hook. Where its neck met Ratsey's shoulders, blood and green slime seemed to be oozing out.

But if the mask had been designed to frighten Hawkins, this time it hadn't worked. Quickly, he brought the horse under control, then called out, "What do you want?"

"Your money!" Ratsey replied, his voice muffled behind the mask. "All of it. Your horse also. Your clothes. I like the look of your boots. And I think, while I'm at it, I may also take your life!"

Hawkins said nothing. He jumped down from the horse, leaving Tom feeling very lost and alone. Ratsey glanced up, the blank fish eyes gazing at him. "Tom-Tom!" he exclaimed.

"You know the boy?" Hawkins demanded.

"Know him? Why, he and I are old mates. Drinking friends. And partners in crime."

Hawkins glanced back at Tom, uncertain for the first time. "You knew he would be here?" he asked.

"I tried to warn you," Tom answered, miserably.

"Tried to warn him, Tom-Tom?" Ratsey shook his head. "Tut! Tut! That's not loyal. That's not nice. But enough of this idle chat. Let's kill this fellow, whoever he is, and then we can ride back together…"

But Hawkins had planted his feet firmly on the ground. He threw back his cloak, revealing his sword. He turned again to Ratsey. "Whatever you may say," he said, "this boy isn't with you. You and he are as different as night and day. I'm taking him with me. And I warn you now to let us pass…"

"Please, Ratsey!" Tom called out, though he knew it was useless. He couldn't even see Ratsey's face but he knew that it would be as emotionless as the dead-fish mask. And he was right.

"Please, Ratsey!" The highwayman echoed the words in a mocking falsetto voice.

Hawkins unsheathed his sword with a great flourish, the metal whispering against the leather scabbard.

Ratsey raised the weapon he was carrying and fired.

It was an arquebus, a type of musket. Tom had never seen such a thing before, never heard anything as loud as the explosion it made. At first he wasn't even sure what had happened. It seemed to him that Hawkins had thrown his own weapon away. Then the traveller turned and to Tom's horror, there was a great hole in the centre of his chest and blood was pouring out, soaking down into his trousers, draining out of him even as Tom watched. Behind him, Ratsey had lowered his gun and was muttering something but Tom, his ears still ringing, couldn't hear him. Smoke curled up from the muzzle of the arquebus. Hawkins staggered towards him.

"To London," he rasped. "Go to Moorfield..." He lifted a hand and with the last of his strength brought it down hard on the horse's rump. Tom felt the horse leap forward and flailed out, searching for something to hold on to. Somehow his fingers found the horse's mane and he knotted them into it. Out of the corner of his eye he saw William Hawkins collapse, lifeless, to the ground. And there, right in front of him, was Ratsey, the fish mask already off his head and his handsome eyes staring at him with something like disbelief.

"Tom-Tom!" he called out.

Tom couldn't have stopped the horse even if he had wanted to. The next thing he knew, the two of them had left the ground, and soared over Ratsey. Ratsey yelled and dived to one side as the horse just missed him, its hind hooves grazing the side of his face. Tom was yelling too. He seemed to be flying. Then there was a great crash as the horse hit the ground again and if Tom's hands hadn't been buried in the mane he would have been torn loose

46

from the saddle. Even so the breath was punched out of him and it felt as if every bone in his body had been rattled loose. Slipping first one way, then the other, he desperately clung on as the horse thundered through the wood, swerving past the trees, leaving its dead master in the mud behind.

As the sun set that evening, three people sat round a table in the Pig's Head. None of them were speaking. They had not spoken for an hour.

Sebastian Slope was smoking a pipe that smelled of old straw. The reason for this was that it was actually filled with old straw – he had run out of tobacco. Next to him, Henrietta Slope was sipping a tankard of ale, a noisy business lacking, as she did, lips. Opposite them, Gamaliel Ratsey was reading a letter by the light of a candle. He had read it several times already and taken notes but the contents still puzzled him.

"So what does it say?" Henrietta demanded at last. "It's only two pages. It can't be that difficult."

"Actually it's in Latin," Ratsey replied. "It's also in code." He set the pages down. "The letter contains orders," he explained. "The traveller was a knight. Sir William Hawkins. A member of the Gentlemen Pensioners."

"The what?"

Ratsey sighed again. "You really do know nothing about the outside world, do you?" he said. "The Gentlemen Pensioners are the Queen's personal bodyguard. They're closer to the Queen than probably anyone else."

"What? You mean…?" Sebastian had gone completely white. It looked as if he was going to be sick and sure enough a few moments later he was. "Do you mean the Queen sent him?" he continued, when he had recovered.

"The Queen or someone close to her. Yes." Ratsey nodded. "Hawkins was sent to find a boy, the son of Robert the Falconer. Somehow he knew that Tom was the boy. His orders were to carry the boy to London and await further instructions. And that, of course, is where they were heading when Hawkins and I met – so unfortunately for him."

"The Queen!" Sebastian Slope was having trouble breathing. His entire face was like a slice of damp cheese. "If Hawkins was a member of the Mental Intentioners…"

"The Gentlemen Pensioners…"

"If he was working for the Queen, there'll be questions. I mean, when he doesn't show up. They'll send constables. And worse."

"They'll hang us all," Henrietta whispered. Her fingers fluttered to her throat. "Hanged by the neck!"

"They'll probably draw and quarter us first," Ratsey remarked.

"Oh Gawd!" Henrietta turned round and was as sick as her husband had been a few moments before.

"It wasn't us!" Slope exclaimed. "We didn't kill him!" He jerked his pipe in the direction of Ratsey. "It was you! You shot him in the forest!"

For the first time, Ratsey's eyes grew dark. He was still smiling, but suddenly there was a chill in the room. The candle flame flickered and black shadows slithered across his face. "Whatever happens, let's remember one thing," he said in a low voice. "We're in this together. If one of us goes down, we all do. If they're going to build a scaffold, it'll be a scaffold for three."

"They can't tie us in with him," Henrietta whispered. "Hawkins came here. And he left again. What happened after that nobody knows."

"Nobody except the boy," Ratsey said.

There was a long silence.

"Young Tom saw everything," Ratsey continued after a while. "He knows all about us. And if the Queen or her advisers were ever to get their hands on him, that could be very difficult for us."

"Where is he?" Sebastian snapped. "You had him! You let him go! This is all your fault, Ratsey."

Ratsey sighed again. He closed his eyes.

Opened them. Then lashed out with his fist, catching Sebastian right on the nose. "We're all in this together," he went on. "And it seems to me that the one thing we have to do, the only thing we *can* do, is find young Tom."

"How are we going to do that?" Sebastian wailed. Henrietta took out a filthy handkerchief and offered it to him. Both the Slopes looked miserable and terrified.

"We know he's heading for London," Ratsey said in a reasonable tone of voice. "I'll follow him there. I'll find him and I'll kill him."

"You'll never find him in London," Sebastian gasped. "It's a huge place. A vast place. I went there once with my dad to do the Christmas shopping. It was horrible. We'd only been there a few hours and he got murdered. He didn't even have time to get me a present!"

"It is a big place," Ratsey agreed. "But I know people. And the people know people. If the boy is there, I'll know it soon enough." He got to his feet. "I'll see you two love-birds in about a month," he said. "And don't worry about Tom. The boy's as good as dead."

AT THE RED LION

Three days after he had left Framlingham, Tom lost his horse, his food and almost his life.

He had been riding hard and had stopped for the night in a small wood just outside a village. He had been too nervous to go into the village itself. He was travelling outside his parish without a licence and knew that if he was caught he would be flogged. And if they decided he was a beggar or a thief – and how else would a boy like him have his own horse? – they might burn a hole in his ear or slit his nostrils and brand him on the side of his cheek.

And so he was on his own, asleep on a bed of leaves when the three men came. A foot breaking a branch near his head woke him. But he was quick-thinking enough to keep his eyes closed.

"Look at the horse!" a voice whispered.

"It's a beauty!" whispered a second.

"Take it! Take it! And cut the boy's throat!" That was a third voice, slithering out of the night.

"No need to kill him," the first voice replied. "He's asleep…"

"Then take the horse."

"I've got it!"

"Quick…"

And then they were gone.

Tom sat up, shivering. It had been a close escape. If he had so much as opened his eyes, a knife would have been the last thing he would have seen.

It was harder after that. For two whole days he walked. The rain never stopped and soon he felt as if the water were going right through him. He had no food. After twenty-four hours his head was spinning and he could barely see the road ahead. At the start of his journey, he had done his best to avoid people. Now it was the other travellers who avoided him. He was a doomed, half-frozen boy, dying on his feet. Nobody wanted to come near.

On the sixth day, just after the sun had set, Tom came to a town. At least, he assumed it must be a town. He had never seen so many tall and solid buildings so close together.

The first of these was an inn. It was three floors high, its windows ablaze with light and flaming torches in front of the main door. The front of the inn was a brilliant pattern of black beams and white panels with a wooden balcony running all the way along the front. A cobbled pathway led underneath a wide arch and into an inner courtyard and even as Tom watched a great carriage arrived, pulled by four horses, and rattled under and in. Immediately two ostlers appeared, dressed in brown aprons, and ran forward to help the passengers dismount. At the same time, a huge man with a black beard appeared, laughing at nothing in particular and chewing what looked like a leg of lamb. Somehow Tom knew that this was the landlord.

"Welcome, welcome!" the man bellowed. "Everyone is welcome at the Red Lion of Enfield. Come in! Come in!"

Tom watched as the new arrivals went in, laughing and chattering amongst themselves. For a moment he swayed on his feet. He had no more strength left. If this was London, then London would be where he would die. He took a deep breath. His position was hopeless. He had nothing to lose. With the last of his strength, he forced himself across the road. The innkeeper had just seen the last of the guests into the building when he noticed Tom, covered in mud from head to foot and looking more like a broken-down scarecrow than a thirteen-year-old boy.

The innkeeper frowned. "What do you want?" he demanded.

"Please, sir..." Tom had to concentrate to make his lips move. "Can I work for you?"

"Work for me? What the devil makes you think I need a young cozener like you? What work do you want? What work can you do?"

"I can look after the horses, sir. I worked at an inn. In Framlingham..."

"Framlingham?" The innkeeper's eyes narrowed. "That's a long way from here. Run away have you? Do you know what happens to the cursed clapperdudgeons who run away from their masters?"

Tom was too tired to argue. He turned round and was about to leave when the innkeeper grabbed hold of him and yelled out, "Quickly!"

The door opened and a plump, fair-haired woman dressed in an apron and cap came out. She had a narrow face with a pointed chin and such wide eyes that she seemed to be permanently amazed about everything. "Yes?" she demanded.

"See for yourself, Mistress Quickly," the innkeeper replied. "This young apple-squire is asking for work!"

Quickly – for it seemed that was her name – glanced at Tom with distaste. "He's more mud than boy," she remarked. "In fact he's a muddy disgrace."

"Then you deal with him," the innkeeper exclaimed. "The little moon-man wants to work. So give him work. Hard work and plenty of it."

Tom allowed himself to be dragged into the Red Lion, his head spinning. He had never been inside a building quite like it. Pewter plates, piled high with food, flashed in front of his eyes being carried to tables. There were pigeons and pastries, eggs and oysters, lamb, beef, pork, and huge, golden chickens. Hundreds of candles burnt in the inn but they were hardly needed with the glow of not one but three fires, turning everything bright red. And the people! Tom had never seen so many people dressed in the finest clothes, talking and laughing as they ate.

"Through here!"

Tom found himself being pushed through a door and suddenly he was in the kitchen – where, of course, he belonged. But, with a heavy heart, Tom knew that he couldn't work. He could barely stand. And when the woman saw he was good for nothing, he would soon be back out in the rain.

"All right," Mistress Quickly exclaimed. "I want you to sit here, child." She gestured at a seat next to a fire. "Your job is to make sure that the fire doesn't go out. Do you understand?"

"Yes." Tom nodded. "I'm to watch the fire."

"You are also to taste *all* the food you are

given. I need to know that it's malicious. I'll ask you to taste a little wine as well, I think. For the same reason. Do you think you can manage all that? Sitting by the fire? Eating and drinking?"

Tom nodded, amazed.

"Good, good, good!" Mistress Quickly beamed. "I'll snatch up with you later." And then she was gone.

Tom couldn't believe his good fortune. He knew of course that these weren't really jobs at all, that the innkeeper and the woman had taken pity on him and had saved him from death by cold and starvation. It was the first time anyone had been kind to him in his entire life and when, a short while later, a smiling girl brought him a plate of meat and bread and a cup of wine, he had to fight to keep the tears from his eyes. After that he slept, half leaning against the wall, the flames from the fire warming his hands and face.

When he awoke something was towering over him. He looked up alarmed, but it was only Mistress Quickly.

"You feeling better?" she asked.

"Yes. Thank you..."

"Please! There's no need to spank me!" She smiled. "Have you ever seen a play?"

"No," Tom replied.

"Then you're in luck. We've got the players in tonight. Come out and see what you think."

The only entertainment Tom had ever seen in Framlingham had been minstrels (usually out of tune) and jugglers. A bear-baiter had once visited the town with an old, half-starved bear. But the sight of the poor animal being stoned and tormented had only made him feel miserable. Another time, a group of players had stayed at the Pig's Head but they hadn't performed – the parish didn't approve of plays. The fact was that Tom had very little idea what a play even was. He doubted he would be able to understand it and thought it would be rather dull.

But when he followed Mistress Quickly into the courtyard, the first thing he heard was roars of laughter from the crowd who now lined the balconies leading round the inside of the inn and who were packed neck-and-neck on the ground below. The players – about a dozen of them – had set themselves up at the far end, using one wall of the inn as the back-drop to a makeshift stage. Torches and candles blazed everywhere turning night into day. And as Tom watched, they acted out their story, turning the Red Lion into another world.

It was a mad story.

The play was about two sets of identical twins, two masters and two servants, who accidentally turned up in the same city. Because they looked exactly the same, the masters kept on confusing the twins and the twins kept on mistaking the masters until everyone was chasing everyone else all around the stage. Tom soon found himself swept up in a way he had never known before. It was as if all his own problems were forgotten. For two hours, William Hawkins, the Slopes and Gamaliel Ratsey simply didn't exist. It was a wonderful feeling, to be so lost in something that nothing else mattered.

If Tom had kept his eyes on the stage like everyone else, he might not have seen what happened next. But he enjoyed watching the audience too – he had never seen so many people having such a good time – and it was while his eyes were on them that he saw the thief at work.

The thief was a boy, a couple of years older than himself. He was wearing a thick red cloak with a tall hat on his head and brown trousers ballooning out at the knees. The boy had a rather round face, long fair hair and thick lips.

The boy was standing right behind a wealthy-looking merchant and, as Tom watched, he reached forward, his hand disappearing underneath the man's cloak. At the same time, his other hand drew out a short sword and cut through the man's purse. Tom gasped. It had taken less than five seconds and now the purse was in the boy's pocket and he was already moving on to the next person in the crowd.

Mistress Quickly was standing next to Tom. "What is it?" she demanded.

"There! He took that man's purse!" Tom lifted his hand and pointed at the boy. At that very moment, the boy looked up at Tom. And to Tom's astonishment, his face broke into a broad smile.

But Mistress Quickly wasn't amused. "A foist!" she yelled. "There's a pock-picket in the house!"

At once the play was forgotten as the audience exploded. They knew there was a thief among them. The only trouble was, they didn't know who he was.

"There!" Mistress Quickly shouted again.

The thief took one last glance at Tom. Slowly he shook his head as if to reproach Tom for spoiling his fun. Then he pointed at a fat, bald man two rows behind him. "That's him!" the thief cried out.

"What...?" the bald man began, then yelled as someone punched him full on the nose. The bald man reeled back, blood flying, then crashed into two more members of the audience. This sparked off a second fight and moments later the entire audience was shouting and swearing, exchanging blows and sprawling over the courtyard. On the stage, the actors tried to continue the scene, realized it was hopeless and stopped to watch. Now it was the actors who had become the audience and the audience who provided the entertainment. Just in front of the stage, two men began a sword fight. A very old lady lashed out with a surprisingly strong fist. A merchant had the shirt ripped off his shoulders while two more grappled with each other's beards.

Tom looked down at the battlefield, searching for the boy who had started it all. A moment later he saw him. The boy had reached the archway and was slipping out into the street. The boy looked back and saw Tom. He took out his stolen purse and raised it in a defiant gesture, then drew a quick finger across his nose. His meaning was clear. To hell with you! To hell with you all!

Then the boy turned and a moment later he had gone.

PAUL'S WALK

The following morning, Mistress Quickly and the innkeeper said their goodbyes. There was a cart making the short journey from Enfield to London and they had arranged for Tom to be given a ride.

"You look after yourself, young rakehell!" the innkeeper boomed. "And when you get to London, make sure you head for St Paul's."

"Where's that?" Tom asked.

"St Paul's Cathedral. You can't miss it. Ask for Paul's Walk. That's the best place to find work."

"Goodbye!" Mistress Quickly cried. "It was lovely beating you!"

The cart set off and although Tom had slept well the night before, he found his eyes closing once again and soon he had drifted back into sleep.

He was woken by the sound of a bell tolling.

He sat up and blinked. The cart was rumbling past a priory with a cluster of neat houses lying in its shadow and at first Tom thought he was still in the countryside. Behind him there were fields and gently sloping hills. But when he twisted round and looked ahead, more and more houses and shops sprang up and a moment later he knew that they had plunged into the city itself.

London!

It was the noise that struck him first. There were people everywhere, shouting and shoving as they tried to reach the market stalls. At the same time, the stall-owners and shopkeepers were shouting back at them, each one of them trying to make themselves heard. "What do you lack? What do you lack?" – this from the shopkeepers, standing in their doorways. "Sweep! Chimney sweep!" "Ripe apples red!" "Fine Seville oranges" – at every street corner there was someone with something to sell.

Horses stamped and stumbled in the mud. Cartwheels creaked and rattled. Dogs barked and cows bellowed their protest as they were driven to market. In workshops open to the street, half-naked metalworkers smashed down with their hammers and yelled instructions to their hurrying apprentices. Carpenters in leather aprons sawed and chiselled. A group of sailors wove past, half-drunk already, singing and laughing. So much noise! Tom pressed his hands to his ears and tried to stop his head from spinning.

And then there was the smell. Vegetables and spices in the market. Fruit – fresh and rotting. Great hunks of cheese. Kegs of rich, ruby wine. The smell of people, sweating and dirty. The smell of animals. And, of course, the worst smell of all, coming from an open drain that ran down the centre of the road, a foul-coloured stream that never stopped flowing, carrying all the sewage of London to who could say where!

Tom climbed out of the cart, marvelling at all the people around him. Colourful signs hung in the air, advertising the shops below. A black horse, a white rose, a yellow snake. Higher up, the inhabitants had stretched lines from one side of the street to the other so that they could hang out their clothes which fluttered like misshapen flags against the blue sky. A woman in expensive clothes hurried past, pressing a scent-bottle to her nose and trying not to look at anything. In the distance a group of boys were throwing mud-balls and laughing at a man with dark skin and foreign-looking clothes; presumably a visitor.

"Dirty postcard?" A man with a broken nose, several broken teeth and a badly twisted neck had suddenly stepped in front of Tom. "Want to buy a dirty postcard?" he asked.

"No..."

"Each one's engraved! And you won't find a filthier sonnet!"

"No thank you!"

The innkeeper had advised Tom to go to St Paul's Cathedral and that at least was easy to find. The driver of the cart pointed the way and Tom followed a narrow, curving lane until it suddenly opened into a great square where a priest, dressed in black and white, was addressing a crowd of a hundred people. The cathedral stood behind them; a mountain of bricks and stone, of soaring windows and towers. Tom wouldn't have believed it was possible to build anything as big as this. The main tower seemed almost to touch the sky – and surely would have if only it hadn't managed to lose its steeple.

He went inside.

It was almost noon and St Paul's was beginning to empty. Tom walked slowly up the central aisle, its great stone pillars standing like some enchanted forest all around him. A door slammed shut and the sound echoed through the chamber. There were a few men lounging against the pillars. Some were talking in low voices. In the shadows, one man was counting coins into the outstretched palm of another. Everyone in the church seemed to be watching someone else and it occurred to Tom that nobody was actually praying.

He reached a tall, wooden door, covered

from top to bottom with slips of paper. A handful of men had been examining these as Tom approached but now they dispersed and he found himself alone. The pieces of paper were covered with words. Tom recognized a few of the letters but, of course, he couldn't read.

"What are you looking for, my dear boy?"

The speaker was a small, fat man, almost as round as he was tall. He reminded Tom of a snowman. His eyes were as black as coal. His nose was long and pointed. And his head seemed to balance on his shoulders without the benefit of a neck. He was wearing black trousers and a white shirt, frayed at the elbows. The fur on his collar looked suspiciously like rat.

"What?" Tom wasn't even sure that the man was talking to him.

"You're new in town." The man smiled. His lips were wet and rubbery. "I haven't seen you here before."

"I only got here today." Tom was afraid to give any information away. He had taken an immediate dislike to the man without quite knowing why.

But the man seemed unaware of it. "You've come to the right place," he said. "My name is Grimly. James Grimly at your service!" He tried to bow but his stomach was too round and didn't have anywhere to bend. "So you are looking for work?"

"I might be…"

"How nice." The man ran his eyes over Tom rather as if he were inspecting a horse or a piece of meat. "If you were – that is – looking for work," he went on, "I might be able to help."

"How?"

"I have a large number of people in my employment. Young lads like yourself. James Grimly's boys are well-known on the streets of London."

"What sort of work do they do?" Tom asked, feeling more uneasy by the minute.

"It's charity work," Grimly explained. He giggled. "Yes. There are people, you see, who need to give to charity. And so it follows that there must be people who *are* charity. That's what I supply. That's my boys."

Tom didn't quite understand this, nor did he like it. "Thank you, Mr Grimly," he said. "But I don't think I'm interested."

"Your choice, my dear fellow. Of course it is! Maybe soon you'll change your mind. But for now I leave you to dine with Duke Humphrey!"

Tom frowned, not knowing what he meant.

Grimly pointed at a large, stone tomb. "Humphrey, Duke of Gloucester!" he explained. "No money? No food? Then you're on your own with him!" The little man

66

laughed and walked away, his boots clattering on the stone floor.

Relieved to see him go, Tom turned and was about to go back the way he had come when he stopped and froze.

The main door must have opened and closed while he was talking to Grimly. A man had come in and was talking to another cluster of men, asking them questions. Even from a distance, Tom recognized his long black hair, his slim, languid body, his penetrating blue eyes. Gamaliel Ratsey had followed him to London. Somehow he had overtaken him on the road. If he so much as raised his head, he would see him. Tom knew he had to hide.

He looked the other way. James Grimly had almost reached the far door and before he knew quite what he was doing, Tom had caught up with him. Grimly's snowball head swivelled on his shoulders. He didn't look surprised to see Tom.

"My dear boy!" he said. "My most likeable fellow! Do I take it that you've changed your mind?"

"Yes," Tom blurted out. "I have." He was almost whispering, afraid that Ratsey would hear him even though he was right on the other side of the cathedral.

"Then let's hurry to my offices before you change your mind again," Grimly said. "We'll have to prepare you for your work. It will mean certain ... changes. The sooner it's done, the sooner you can start."

Tom nodded, although he had heard little of what the man had said.

Leaving Paul's Walk behind them, the two set off together.

Grimly had a yard at the end of a dark, narrow alleyway near the Thames. The city was much quieter here, with fewer people on the streets and a damp, evil-smelling fog in the air. Slimy water and mud rose over Tom's ankles as the two of them hurried towards a pair of mouldering wooden gates.

"My home," Grimly muttered. He opened the gates and ushered Tom inside. The gates led into a rough, partly cobbled courtyard, squeezed between three buildings that seemed to be leaning on each other to stay upright. Tom looked around him. Set in the middle of the courtyard was a single, wooden chair with a high back and solid arms and legs. Tom had no idea what the chair was for. But there was something about it that made him go cold inside.

"Belter!" Grimly called. "Snivel! Get the book! Get out here! We have a new recruit!"

Almost at once a door at the side of the courtyard flew open and two men hurried out. The first of these, the man called Belter, was huge and muscular, completely bald with a face that hadn't quite formed, like an over-sized baby. He was naked to the waist. He had no hair on his chest and his nipples were black. Snivel was older, a crumpled bag of a man, carrying a leather-bound book underneath his withered arm.

"A new recruit?" Snivel rasped. He licked his lip. "From Paul's Walk?" he asked.

"Where else?" Grimly turned to Tom. "We'll prepare you straight away."

"Prepare me?" Tom was getting more nervous by the second. "What do you mean?"

"I thought I told you. It's for charity!"

"Charity!" Snivel agreed.

"What sort of charity?" Tom demanded.

Grimly sighed. "The homeless and the disabled," he explained. "I've got boys all over London. On street corners. Outside churches. They're Grimly's boys."

"You mean they're beggars!"

"Exactly. But they're special beggars. They work for me and I take half of what they earn. But in return I help them, you see. I *adjust* them." Grimly flicked a finger in Tom's direction. "Take a boy like you. You're a little thin. A little ragged. But how much do you think that's worth? Good people, charitable people, people with money ... they want something more. Oh yes, they might give a penny to a child shivering with cold. But how much do you think they'd give to that same child, *missing a leg*?"

Grimly had barely spoken the last three words before Tom was running for the gate. But Belter had been expecting it. Before Tom had taken two paces he was grabbed from behind and dragged, screaming to the wooden chair. There was nothing he could do as he was forced down, his hands and feet securely fastened with rope. It was over in a matter of seconds. By the time the giant had finished with him Tom was sitting helplessly, unable to move.

"Let me go!" he shouted. "I've changed my mind! I don't want to work for you!"

Grimly touched a finger to his lips. "Don't shout," he said in a soft, soothing voice. "It won't hurt that much."

Belter had produced a dirty canvas bag from somewhere. He dropped it on the cobbled ground and Tom heard it clink.

"Now what shall we do with him?" Grimly asked. "How about one arm and one leg?"

Snivel had opened his book. "We did one of those last week," he said.

"All right then. Just the legs." Grimly smiled at Tom. "He's a handsome fellow. Interesting hair colour. Nice eyes. Let's leave the top half alone."

Belter grabbed hold of him and Tom screamed.

Then the doors of the yard crashed open.

70

Tom was too far gone to understand fully what was happening but he became dimly aware that Belter had straightened up again and that Grimly was walking forward with a look of annoyance on his face. "You!" he exclaimed. "What are you doing here?"

Tom forced his head to turn so that he could see the new arrival. A boy a couple of years older than himself was standing by the open door, leaning against the wall and smoking a pipe. He was looking at the scene with what could only be described as an amused smile. Tom thought he had seen the boy somewhere before but he knew that was impossible.

"Let the boy go," the new arrival demanded.

"What?" Grimly looked more sad than angry. "But he came here of his own choice," he protested. "I found him at Paul's Walk..."

"Oh yes! And you explained to him all about your little 'adjustments' I'm sure. Just like all the others!"

"Wait a minute! Wait a minute! We can talk about this...!"

Out of the corner of his eye, Tom saw Snivel reaching into a fold in his shirt. While Grimly prattled on, the old man's hand inched out and now it was holding a wicked-looking knife. Tom opened his mouth to call out a warning to the boy but there was no need. In a single movement he swept back his cloak to reveal a short sword which was suddenly out of its scabbard and in his hand, slicing through the air. The blade caught the edge of the knife, tore it out of Snivel's hand and sent it spinning through the air to clatter harmlessly on the ground. Then the point of the boy's sword was at Grimly's throat, pressing against the skin.

"Please!" Grimly's black eyes bulged. A bead of sweat trickled over his neck. "This is just business. It's nothing to do with you. He's my boy. I found him."

The boy shook his head and pressed a little harder with the sword. "Not this one, Grimly. He's a friend of mine. Let him go."

A *friend of mine*? So Tom was right. He had seen the boy somewhere before. But where?

Grimly had one last try. "But look at him!" he moaned. "Nice face. Intelligent eyes. But sad with it. We were just going to take off his legs. He'll earn a fortune."

"Maybe," the boy replied. "But you won't be alive to see it." His hand tightened on the sword. "I've often thought London would be better off without you, Grimly," he said. "All I need is the excuse..."

"No! Take him!" Grimly was on the edge of tears and his voice was a whisper. Belter and Snivel ran forward and a few seconds later the ropes had fallen away and Tom was able to stand up.

"This way..." the boy said. He had lowered

his sword but his eyes never left the three men.

Tom staggered over to him and he and the boy left the yard together. It was only when they had reached the end of the alley and emerged into the main street that he realized two things.

The first thing was that he *did* know the boy. He had seen him the night before at the Red Lion, stealing a purse in the middle of the play.

And the second thing was that he wasn't a boy at all. He might be wearing trousers, carrying a sword and smoking a pipe, but Tom had just been rescued by a girl!

MOLL CUTPURSE

"My name," she said, "is Moll Cutpurse."

"Cutpurse?" Tom frowned. "Is that your real name?"

"One of them. I've got lots." Moll thought for a moment. "I used to be called Mary but I soon put a stop to that. Much too girlish." She rubbed her chin as if hoping to find stubble there. "You wouldn't want to be a girl," she said. "Not in the sixteenth century!"

"What do you do?" Tom asked.

"What do you think I do?" Moll exclaimed. "I'm a thief. A highly qualified thief. In fact, I came top in my class!"

She and Tom were sitting in a small, square room above a shoe shop. The building was perched on the south bank of the river, so close that Tom could hear the water lapping against the brickwork. The single room contained a bed, two chairs, a table, a cupboard and a small fire that struggled to keep out the damp. However, the windows had glass. The roof didn't leak. And, as Moll was quick to point out, it didn't have rats.

She had warmed up some stew over the fire and served it on two thick slices of bread – she had no plates. Somewhere she had found a bottle of wine. Now the two of them were gazing at each other over the table.

"Do you have parents?" Tom asked.

"My father used to run the shoe shop downstairs," Moll replied. "But he died of the plague. My mother too. I think I had a brother but he disappeared. Anyway, I'm on my own now."

There was a long silence. Moll leant forward and put another log on the fire. The flames reached out tiredly to consume it.

"I suppose you want to know how I found you," Moll said.

"Yes."

"It was just luck, really. I was at Paul's Walk. I go there. Everyone does. I saw you meet up with Grimly and I followed you."

"But why? Why did you save me?"

"Because I wanted to kill you myself."

Tom stared. Moll was still wearing her sword and he waited for her to draw it – but her hands didn't move.

"You cost me plenty at the Red Lion," she went on. "I'd never seen so many purses. I'd have had a dozen of them if it hadn't been for you. And you could have got me hanged!"

"I'm sorry."

"It's a bit late for that now."

Tom gestured at the sword. "So why haven't you?" he asked. "Killed me, I mean."

Moll shrugged. "Because if you were stupid enough to go off with James Grimly you were probably too stupid to know what you were doing at the Red Lion. Anyway, don't ask too many questions or I may change my mind."

There was a brief silence.

"Thank you for rescuing me," Tom said.

"That's all right." Moll took a sip of wine. "The question is – what do I do with you?"

"Can I stay here?"

"No!" Moll sighed. "All right. One night. Maybe two. But I don't like boys. Particularly stupid boys who don't know what they're doing. What *are* you doing? I suppose you're a runaway. Left your master, have you?"

"I didn't run away. It wasn't like that."

"Then what was it like? You might as well tell me. Not that I'm offering to help…"

So Tom told her his story; about his life with the Slopes and Gamaliel Ratsey; the arrival of William Hawkins and the ambush in the forest; Moll's eyes narrowed when she heard Ratsey's name and when Tom told her he had seen Ratsey at Paul's Walk she shook her head doubtfully. "You know him?" Tom asked.

"I've heard of him. Everyone's heard of Ratsey. But it's unlike him to be down here in London. And I think it's bad news for you."

"That's what I thought," Tom agreed.

"He's dangerous. As long as he's here, you're in danger. He'll find you soon enough. And when he does..." Moll drew a finger across her throat.

"That's very encouraging," Tom muttered.

Moll thought for a moment. "Tell me more about Hawkins," she said.

"I've told you everything I know."

"That's the bit of your story that doesn't make sense." Moll took out her pipe and lit it. "He was obviously a gentleman. Maybe even a member of the court. He asks questions about you and about your parents and then he snatches you and brings you back here."

"He said I should go to Moorfield."

"But why? What did he want with you? I mean, you're a nobody. A nothing. A stable boy who barely knows one end of a horse from the other..."

"Thanks!"

"And why Moorfield?" Moll sighed and blew out a perfect smoke ring. "I suppose I could take you there."

"You know where it is?"

"Of course I do. It's just outside the city wall. We could walk there in half an hour. But I wouldn't get too excited if I were you.

There's nothing there. A few butts. Some windmills. If that's what he brought you all this way to see, he was wasting your time."

"Maybe he lived there."

"Nobody smart lives in Moorfield. How do you think it got its name? It used to be a moor. Now it's a field."

"At least we can look," Tom said, gloomily.

Moll nodded. "All right. We'll look. But it's too late to go there now. The sun will be down in an hour or so. We'll go there tomorrow morning."

"What about tonight?" Tom looked around the room. "You said I could stay here?"

"Yes."

"But there's only one bed."

"No problem. You can have the floor."

From the moment he had walked into Moll's room, Tom had felt that he was being watched. But it was only later that night, as he lay on the floor with a single blanket and the flickering fire to keep him warm, that he realized who by. The room looked out, not just on to the river but also on to London Bridge. The huge bridge with its twenty stone arches and its shops, houses and chapels all crammed together above the water, was one of the great sights of the city.

But as he gazed at it in the moonlight, Tom noticed something else. There *were* three heads turned towards the window, three pairs of eyes fixed on him even now. But they were eyes that saw nothing. The heads they belonged to ended at the neck, cut off and stuck on metal poles.

Traitors. This was the price they had paid.

Tom rolled over and pulled the blanket over his head. But he could still feel the eyes boring into him. And it was a long, long time before he lost himself in the brief escape of sleep.

Moll was right about Moorfield.

She and Tom were standing in a rectangular field, just north of the city wall. Far away to the north, Tom could just make out the shape of three windmills. There were a few cattle grazing here and there. Despite the icy weather – it seemed to be getting colder by the day – a handful of people had come out to practise archery, aiming at two straw-filled targets, the "butts" that Moll had mentioned. It was a sunny day but the sun was white, not yellow, and gave no warmth at all. Somewhere, dogs were barking. Otherwise, Moorfield was empty and silent.

"Seen enough?" Moll asked.

"Yes."

"Maybe you didn't hear him properly. Maybe he didn't want to bring you here."

"He definitely said Moorfield."

Moll shrugged. "Let's go and get a drink," she said. "I'm freezing!"

They turned south and went through Moorgate, back into the city. That was the strange thing about London. It was huge, crowded, the streets and houses jammed into what little space there was between the wall and the river. But walk ten minutes in almost any direction and suddenly you had left it all behind and you were back in the countryside. It was a city surrounded by green.

Moll led Tom into a tavern, took the table nearest the fire and ordered two pints of ale. Neither of them spoke until it came. At last Moll lit her pipe and broke the silence. "So what are you going to do now?" she asked.

Tom was feeling more miserable than ever. In all the time he had been travelling from Framlingham and despite what Moll had said the night before, he had been hoping that Moorfield would mean something, be something. That when he got there everything would make sense. But a field, a handful of cows and three windmills? Why should Hawkins have brought him all the way from Framlingham for that?

"I don't know," he said.

"Maybe you should get out of London. If you've got Ratsey looking for you!"

"But where will I go?" Tom cried. "I haven't got anywhere."

"I'm told Bristol's nice. You could join the navy."

"I'd get sea-sick," Tom said.

"How about the army?"

"That's worse. I'd get shot."

Moll slammed down her tankard. "I knew it was a mistake coming after you," she muttered. "Now I'm stuck with you. A boy! The last thing I need!"

"Maybe I could learn how to be a thief ... like you?" Tom suggested. But even as he spoke the words, he knew it wouldn't work. Tom lived in a world where there were as many thieves as honest men. He had spent his entire life surrounded by them. He knew that many people had a simple choice. Steal or starve. But even so, there was something inside him that told him that stealing was wrong and that it wouldn't work for him. His heart would never be in it.

Moll must have sensed this because she shook her head. "No."

"Then what?"

"Listen to me." Moll leaned forward. "If you are going to stay in London, you've got to go somewhere where Ratsey won't find you. And that means you can't stay with me, even if I wanted you to. Everyone knows everyone down here. Paul's Walk isn't just a meeting place. It's where everyone finds out about everyone else. That's why he was there yesterday and that's why he'll be there today." Moll looked nervously over her shoulder. "We've been in here half an hour," she went on, "and who knows who's seen us together? Someone could be on their way to Ratsey even now. You stay with me, he'll find you soon enough. Believe me. You won't be safe with me."

Tom nodded, feeling gloomier by the minute.

"We have to find you work. You need money in your pocket and a roof over your head."

"But what sort of work can I do?"

"That's a good question." Moll thought for a minute. "I could get you into a tavern. You say you've handled horses and there are people I know. No…" She shook her head. "Forget it. Ratsey knows your past and that's the first place he'll look. He's probably checking out every tavern in town even as we sit."

Tom said nothing.

"All right." Moll pointed with her pipe. "We need to get you a job so let's consider your qualifications. Can you cook?"

"No."

"Can you read?"

"No."

"Can you sew?"

"No."

"Can you sing?"

"I've never tried."

Moll sighed. "A typical boy. Completely useless. All right. There's nothing you *can* do. But is there anything you *want* to do? At least that might be worth a try."

82

Tom thought hard. What did he want to do? Here he was in London, the greatest city in the world. He could be anything he wanted to be. But what *did* he want to be? Not a thief. Not a beggar. Could he work in the market? No. He would never make himself heard in all that din. How about a shop assistant? No. That would mean handling money and he couldn't count.

And then he remembered. He had only ever been completely happy once in his entire life. For just a few brief hours all his problems had been forgotten and it was as if he had been transported to another world. At that moment, Tom knew that there was only one thing he wanted to be. He wanted to join the people he had seen two nights before, at the Red Lion of Enfield.

"I know what I want to do, Moll," he said. "I want to join the theatre. I want to act."

AUDITIONS

"I still think it's a stupid idea," Moll said.

"But you don't like the theatre," Tom replied.

"I love the theatre! I go there all the time."

"Yes. But only to rob the audiences."

It was six o'clock in the morning, two days after their unsuccessful visit to Moorfield. Tom was still lying on the floor, wrapped in a blanket, but Moll was already up and fully dressed – which was hardly surprising as she slept in her clothes.

The day before, she had visited Paul's Walk and come back with exciting news. An advertisement had been posted on the *Si Quis* door (this was the name of the door that Tom had himself noticed). Actors were wanted for a new play that was about to be performed at the Rose Theatre, not far from where Moll lived. Those interested were to present themselves at the theatre where auditions would be taking place.

And now it was the day of the auditions. Tom had barely slept a wink the night before. It was a strange thing. He had never once in his entire life thought about becoming an actor. But now he had made the decision, there was nothing he wanted more. It was as if it had been in his blood all along but had only now bubbled to the surface.

Moll was holding a package, wrapped in paper. "This is for you."

Tom threw the blanket off and sat up. "What is it?" he asked.

Moll was suddenly uncomfortable. "Don't you even know what it is in four days' time?" she snapped. "It's Christmas Day. So this is your present."

"You went and bought me a present?" Tom was amazed. Nobody had ever bought him anything. Then a nasty thought crossed his mind. "Did you really *buy* it?" he asked.

"I didn't steal it, if that's what you mean. I used my own money."

"But you stole the money..."

"Well. Yes..."

Tom unwrapped the package. Inside was a white shirt, a pair of woollen trousers, a waistcoat and, most wonderful of all, a pair of leather boots. Tom held them, marvelling. He had been barefoot for as long as he could remember. This leather, soft and warm in his hands, was something he had only ever dreamed about. He gazed at her, unbelieving.

"It's probably a complete waste of money," Moll said, "but you can't turn up at the audition looking like a vagabond. Get dressed. We ought to be on our way."

The Rose Theatre was a large, round building, part wood, part plaster and part brick. It stood in what had once been a garden – that was how it got its name. It was still early in the morning, but already a lot of actors had come to audition: men in feathered caps and flowing cloaks, preening themselves like pigeons.

Moll stopped opposite the main door. "Well. Good luck," she said.

"Aren't you coming in?" Tom asked.

"No." She shook her head. "There's always a chance I might get recognized. I did this place last month." She took Tom's hand. "You know where to find me if you need me. But I'm sure you'll get a job. You look like an actor. You've got an actor's eyes."

"Thanks, Moll."

"If they do hire you, come back and see me on Christmas Day. I'm going out to dinner. A bit of a reunion. You might enjoy it."

"I'm sure I'll be back tonight," Tom said.

"I hope not," Moll retorted. "My room's only big enough for one. And your feet smell."

Moll turned and walked away. Tom watched her until she'd gone. Then, taking a deep breath, he crossed the road and went into the Rose.

Tom found himself in a circular space with seats rising in three tiers and surrounding him on all sides. In front of him was a raised stage with two pillars holding up a slanting, tiled roof. There were two doors at the back, presumably where the actors made their entrances. The theatre had no roof. If it rained (or snowed – the weather was getting colder and colder) the actors and the audience in front of the stage would get soaked. Only the people in the seats would have any chance of staying dry.

There was a man standing in the middle of the stage, reciting what sounded like a poem in a whiny and monotonous voice. Two other men were watching him, sitting on stools to one side. One of these was tall, with dark, curling hair, a beard and tired eyes. The other was shorter and plumper, more expensively dressed with a silk handkerchief draped over his hand.

The actor had only recited about three lines when the bearded man stood up. "That's enough, thank you," he called out. "Next!"

"But I've only just begun!" the actor whined.

"Don't send a messenger to us. We'll send a

messenger to you," the man replied.

The actor left the stage. There was a long line of men snaking round the edge of the theatre. As soon as he had gone, one of them took his place and the line moved forward. Tom walked towards the stage, thrilled and terrified by it at the same time. Could he stand here and perform – perhaps to a hundred or two hundred people?

"Look out!"

With his eyes fixed on the stage, Tom had collided with a young man who had been carrying a sheaf of papers. Now the papers fell out of his hands and cascaded to the floor, some of them carried by the breeze into the very muddiest of puddles. Every page was covered with writing and Tom was horrified to see the words blur and then disappear in a black haze as they came into contact with the water.

"I'm sorry! I'm really sorry..."

Tom did his best to scoop the pages out of the puddle and hand them back to the man.

"Why couldn't you look where you were going?"

"I was looking at the stage. I'm sorry." Tom straightened up, feeling wretched. Here he was in his brand new clothes and already he had made a complete idiot of himself.

The man glanced at him and softened. "It's all right," he said. "I wasn't looking either. I was thinking about my new play."

Tom looked at the man more carefully. He was in his late twenties, dressed in a black velvet tunic with a high white collar. The man had an unusually intelligent face. His deep brown eyes seemed to look right into you; through you and at you at the same time. His hair, also brown, hung almost down to his neck at the back and sides, but he was already going bald on top.

"A new play?" Tom realized what the man had just said. "Are you a writer?"

"Yes. I suppose I am. As a matter of fact, it's my play they're about to perform here." Tom had picked up the last of the pages and the man wiped it clean using his sleeve and added it to the pile. "My name is Shakespeare," he said. "Bill Shakespeare. Or Will Shakespeare if you like. Or Bill..."

Tom was confused. "Is that with a B or not a B?" he asked.

"B or not a B. B or not a B!" Shakespeare's eyes brightened and he suddenly produced a quill and scribbled something down on one of the pages. "That's rather good," he said. "I might use that."

"What's your play about?" Tom asked, changing the subject. Behind them, the second actor had just been dismissed as brutally as the first. A third actor was taking his place.

"Oh. It's about a Roman general called Titus Andronicus," Shakespeare said. "Actually, it's rather violent. But that's what they want…" He pointed at the two men on the stage. "That's Philip Henslowe. He owns the theatre. The other man is Lord Strange … and what's really strange is that we work for him at all because between you and me he's a complete idiot. All he ever wants is clowns and acrobats." He sighed, then glanced at Tom. "Are you here to audition?" he asked, suddenly.

"Yes."

"Oh, I see." Shakespeare grimaced. "Actually, I'm awfully sorry, but I don't think they're looking for girls."

"I'm not a girl!" Tom said indignantly.

"No, no, no!" Shakespeare laughed. "That's not what I meant. Didn't you know? We don't have girls in the theatre. All the girls' parts are played by boys."

This was something Tom had never known. "Why?" he asked.

"They just are." Shakespeare searched through the pages. "But like I say, there are only two girls in the play and they've both been cast."

"Oh." Tom was disappointed.

"Why do you want to be an actor anyway?" Shakespeare asked. "Have you acted before?"

"No."

"But you've been to a play."

"Only once." Suddenly Tom found himself

telling Shakespeare about the play he had seen at the Red Lion. As he started to describe the plot, he saw Shakespeare smile and a moment later the playwright laughed and slapped him on the back. "There's no need to tell me about the play," he said. "It was the *Comedy of Errors*. I wrote it."

Tom gaped. "You're a great writer," he said.

"No, no, no!" Shakespeare blushed. "I'm only just starting out really. But one day ... who knows?"

Despite his meeting with Shakespeare, Tom was feeling lost and dejected as he left the theatre. The visit had been a complete failure. There were no parts for him in the play. He had nowhere to go, no money and no possessions except the clothes he was wearing.

He was so deep in thought that he didn't notice someone slipping out of the theatre behind him. But as he walked down the road the man hurried after him and caught up.

"Excuse me, young sir." The speaker was short and very dark, with narrow, glinting eyes. He was quite bald, apart from two patches of black hair, one above each ear. He also had a moustache, the hairs curling round on each side of his nose. He was dressed exotically in a rich, multi-coloured tunic with a bright red sash across his chest and a matching red plume in his hat. His trousers were mauve, ballooning out above the knee where they were tied tightly with two black ribbons. His stockings were also red. His feet, which were extremely small, were encased in brightly polished black shoes. "I noticed you in the theatre just now," the man went on. There was something foreign about him. Although his English was perfect, there was the trace of an accent, distant and unrecognizable. "You were hoping to perform in a play?"

"Yes." Tom kept on walking.

The man hurried to keep up, almost dancing on his tiny feet. "Then permit me to introduce myself," he said. "My name is Dr Mobius. You've heard of me? No? No matter…" He coughed delicately. "The truth is that I myself have a theatrical company."

That stopped Tom in his tracks. The man smiled at him. He was wearing some sort of perfume and smelled of flowers and musk. "We call ourselves the Garden Players." He waved a set of fingers heavy with rings. "We have a play we wish to perform and I came to the Rose because I'm looking for a boy."

"What sort of play is it?" Tom's mind was reeling and it was the first thing he could think to ask.

Dr Mobius tweaked his moustache. "It's a comedy," he explained. "A very comical comedy in my opinion. But then, I wrote it. It's

called *The Devil and his Boy*. You see? I play
the devil. But, due to an unfortunate accident,
I find myself in need of a boy."

"And you think…?" Tom tried to make
sense of his thoughts. "What makes you think
I'd be right for the part?" he asked.

Dr Mobius simpered. "I am intuitive," he
said. "That is, I am a very sensitive person. I
can sense talent in a young man like yourself.
The way you carry yourself. The way you
speak. Of course…" He whipped out a handkerchief and brushed an imaginary tear from
his eye, "…if you are not interested…"

"I'm interested!" Tom exclaimed.

"How interesting! Good!" Suddenly he was
businesslike. "It will be three weeks' work. We
will pay you six shillings when the job is done.
You will live with us, with the Garden Players,
and you will receive all food and board." He
paused for breath. "What is your name?" he
asked.

"Tom. Tom Falconer."

"You are alone in London?"

Tom was about to mention Moll, then
thought better of it. She wasn't part of this life.
"Yes," he said.

"Then do we have a deal?"

Tom hesitated for a moment. Somewhere,
deep inside him, Tom knew something was
wrong, that this was simply too good to be
true. After all, the last time he had been offered

work, it had nearly cost him both his legs. But at the same time, it was a job. A roof over his head. Food. And he would be acting in a play!

"It's a deal," he said.

Dr Mobius stretched out his arm to shake hands and it was then that it happened. He must have lost a button because, for a moment, his sleeve fell away from his arm. Looking down, Tom saw the man's dark skin and there, just above the wrist, a strange mark. It was an eye with a cross in it. And it hadn't been drawn there. It had been burned into his flesh.

The man glanced at Tom, then down to his exposed arm. For a moment his eyes flared and he opened his mouth in what was almost a snarl. But then, he forced the smile back on to his face and pulled the sleeve back down. "My sleeve," he said. "These London tailors don't know what they're doing!" He brought his hand back up in front of Tom. "So, Tom Falconer, do we have a deal?"

Tom reached out.

They shook.

THE GARDEN PLAYERS

There were eight men in the company known as the Garden Players, but with Tom that figure was brought up to nine.

Tom had followed Dr Mobius back up the south bank of the river. The sun was still shining brightly but Tom couldn't help but notice something rather strange. Mobius preferred the shadows. Whenever the street widened out – when they crossed Long Southwark, for example – his beady eyes searched for darkened alleyways and hidden entrances. If he saw people coming towards him, he chose another way. And so they barely saw anyone as they followed the Thames, heading east, past London Bridge and on to Bermondsey.

They finally arrived at the river itself and Dr Mobius stopped, blinking in the light. It was snowing now and Tom could see the surface of the Thames beginning to ice over. He wondered how long it would be before he was able to cross it on foot.

"Here we are," Mobius panted, speaking for the first time since they had set off. He waved a hand. "We are here."

"Where…?" Tom began.

The river was lapping at a derelict wooden jetty in front of them. A single ship was moored there, obviously no longer seaworthy. The sails hung in rags from its four masts and there was a gaping hole in its side where the wood seemed to have mouldered away. But there were no buildings close by; no taverns and certainly no theatres.

"The ship, Tom!" Mobius pressed his fingers together. "We hired a ship. A little economy, you understand. We live there. We work – the deck is a perfect stage. We are, if you like, a family afloat. Yes, I like that. The family that floats. And now you are part of our family, Tom. A very welcome part. Please! This way…"

Dr Mobius walked up a half-rotten gangplank and Tom followed.

"This way!" Mobius pointed at a door and a set of steps leading down inside the ship and disappeared. Tom stood for a moment, feeling the deck moving underneath his feet. He had never been on a ship before and had no idea how so much wood and rigging could possibly float when even the smallest stone would sink instantly. But this was no time for such questions. Nervous now, he crossed the deck and went through the door.

There were seven men, sitting in chairs or lying in hammocks around a coal brazier. The room was full of smoke both from the fire and the candles that lit it. Mobius had removed his hat and was helping himself to a glass of sherry from a small wooden cask. "Gentlemen," he said. "Our new boy! Yes! His name is Tom."

The men nodded at Tom and one or two of them smiled. The first thing that Tom noticed was that, like Dr Mobius, they were all rather dark. The oldest of them must have been about forty, the youngest (playing a woman, as it turned out) only a few years older than Tom himself. They were dressed in leather trousers, thick shirts and boots. Sitting there, in the cramped and smoky cabin, they looked more like sailors or soldiers than actors.

Mobius introduced them. "This is Ferdinand. Frederick. Philip. Florian. Francis with an 'i'. Frances with an 'e'. And Fynes." Tom promptly forgot each man's name as he was told it and wondered how he would manage when it came to learning his lines. He was beginning to feel more and more uncomfortable. It wasn't that the men were unfriendly. It was just the way they were looking at him … soft and secretive. He had thought actors would be more cheerful than this.

97

"We must start work!" Mobius exclaimed. "Ferdinand – a script for our new friend."

The men swung off their bunks and moved to sit round a low table in the middle of the cabin. They each had a great bundle of paper and one of them produced a copy which he handed to Tom. It was the moment Tom had been dreading. He turned to Mobius, the blood rushing to his face. "I can't read," he said.

But to his surprise, Mobius merely laughed. "It's no problem! We will help you to learn the lines. And when you have learned the lines you won't need to read."

The youngest actor – Florian – a boy with long, fair hair and sad eyes – sat down next to Tom and took his script. "I will read the lines for you," he said. Like Mobius, he spoke with a slightly foreign accent.

For the next ninety minutes, Tom listened as Mobius and the Garden Players read *The Devil and his Boy*.

The play was, as Mobius had said, a comedy. It was about a man called Lucio (played by Dr Mobius) who had just arrived in the city of Venice and who dressed up as the devil in order to win a bet. Very quickly, though, things got out of hand as the people of Venice came to believe that he was the *real* devil. There was a comical merchant with a beautiful daughter, Isabella, (played by Florian), a comical priest and a comical duke. In fact, everyone in the play was meant to be comical in one way or another. The play ended with the duke and two soldiers, all of them armed with muskets, chasing Lucio and his boy off the stage.

The boy, of course, was Tom's part. He played Antonio, Lucio's servant, but as it turned out this wasn't such a big part after all. Tom appeared in the first three acts and once at the end. His main job was to provide a sort of commentary on the action. "Methinks my master is a scurvy knave" – that sort of thing. But of course he didn't complain. Listening to the actors reading the play, he still found it hard to believe that he was one of them. It did trouble him a little that the play didn't seem to be very good. And it also occurred to him – although of course he couldn't be sure – that not one of these actors could actually act. They all had that strange, very faint foreign accent. And they seemed to be reading their parts with no interest or enthusiasm whatsoever. But it was a start. The Garden Players today. The Rose Theatre tomorrow. At least, that was what Tom told himself.

They reached the end of the fifth act. Florian turned over the last page. There was a moment's pause but nobody applauded or said anything to break the silence.

"So, are there any questions?" Mobius asked.

Tom waited but still nobody spoke. There had been a question he had been meaning to ask from the very start, something that had puzzled him. But for the moment it was out of his mind and he asked instead, "When are we going to perform the play?"

"Soon." Mobius sipped his sherry. "I still have a few little arrangements that have to be, you know, arranged."

"It's a lot to learn." This was Florian who, as Isabella, had one of the largest parts.

"We will work hard." Dr Mobius set down his glass and stared hard at everyone around the table. "From today, none of us leave this ship without my permission. We will rehearse on the deck or – if the snow or the rain of this accursed country makes that impossible – down here. Florian! You will teach Tom his lines. Day and night. We must be ready for our grand opening." He turned to Tom. "From now on, Tom, you are mine. You must remember that. Do as you are told. And take care. We would hate anything accidental to happen to you … accidentally. You understand?"

Suddenly Tom knew what he had meant to ask before. "The boy who was meant to play my part…" He looked up at Mobius. "What happened to him?"

One of the men shifted uncomfortably on his stool. Next to Tom, Florian cast his eyes down and pretended to study the script.

Dr Mobius sighed and spread his hands, his many rings sparkling in the light of the candles. "Poor Frank," he said. "It's exactly what I mean. Yes. Exactly. You see, he tried to leave the ship one night without asking my permission. Somehow he must have slipped ... in the dark, maybe." Dr Mobius laid a hand on Tom's shoulder. He leant down and gazed straight at him. "He fell into the river and drowned. Make sure the same thing doesn't happen to you!"

Rehearsals began that afternoon and for the next three days Tom found himself utterly absorbed in the business of producing a play. Fortunately it had stopped snowing and they were able to rehearse on deck. The play demanded lots of running around, sometimes with guns, sometimes with devil's pitchforks, and Tom wondered how they would ever have managed inside.

Because he relied on Florian to read his lines, he found himself closer to the other boy than to anyone else. The rest of the company were as reserved as they had been when he first met them. They rarely spoke to him. But nor did they often speak to each other. They seemed nervous. He wondered if any of them had ever acted before.

It wasn't easy getting Florian to talk either. As the days passed, he learned that the boy was sixteen years old and that Dr Mobius was his uncle.

"When did you start acting?" Tom asked.

"This is my first play."

"Is it something you always wanted to do?"

"No!" Florian fell silent, his sad eyes turning away. "I just do what my uncle tells me to," he said. "Now stop asking questions and let's go through your lines."

Tom was perplexed. But it was only on his second night on the boat that he saw something that actually disturbed him.

All the actors slept in one room – the same room where they had read the play. This was the only room on the ship that was remotely dry or warm enough, although Dr Mobius had a cabin to himself on the other side of the deck. Tom had a hammock next to Florian, with the actor called Ferdinand (who played the merchant) on the other side. However, on that second night, he couldn't sleep. The weather was colder than ever, the river a solid sheet of ice now. He could feel the chill seeping through the woodwork and into his bones.

Next to him, Ferdinand groaned and turned over. The movement pulled back his shirt sleeve and with a start, Tom saw the man's bare arm. There was an eye with a cross burned into the flesh, between the wrist and the elbow. He had seen exactly the same thing on the arm of Dr Mobius.

Tom straightened up. What did it mean? Were *all* the actors carrying the same mark and, if so, why? Why should they have consented to allow themselves to be branded like animals?

Tom lay back down in his hammock and closed his eyes. But that night he didn't sleep a wink.

Another day came and went. Tom had learned all of Act One and most of Act Two. That only left a short scene in Act Five and he would be ready. But ready for what? Dr Mobius still hadn't said where *The Devil and his Boy* was going to be performed or when. And Tom still hadn't been paid. He had tried asking Florian, but of course without success, and was just summoning up the courage to tackle Dr Mobius himself when the visitor arrived.

It was about four o'clock in the afternoon and already dark, a few flurries of snow gusting against the rotting ship. Tom was watching a scene from Act Four being rehearsed when the man approached the ship. The man was wearing a long brown robe that reached all the way to his feet with a hood drawn over his head. A monk or a friar. The man glanced over his shoulder, then hurried up the gangplank. At that moment, Dr Mobius saw him. "That is, I think, enough for today," he called out, stopping the rehearsal in mid-sentence.

"Please return to your cabin. Yes, I think, to the cabin. While I attend to some ... business."

The monk had stood waiting while Mobius spoke. Then Mobius bowed and gestured to his private quarters on the other side of the deck. Still keeping his face hidden underneath the hood, the monk scuttled across the deck and disappeared through the door. Dr Mobius followed him. The door slammed shut behind them.

The other actors were only too pleased to be released from their work in the cold evening air and crowded round the door in their haste to get back to the fire. Florian went with them and suddenly Tom, who had been sitting alone on the deck above, found himself momentarily forgotten.

His first instinct was to follow the others down. It was extremely cold and the last one in would always find himself furthest from the fire. But at the same time he was curious. Why should a monk have suddenly chosen to visit a company of actors and why should Dr Mobius be so eager to see him? He had to know. And suddenly he had an idea. Perhaps there was a way he could find out.

There was a rope lying on the deck. In fact there were ropes all over the ship but this was the only one that hadn't been gnawed at, either by time or by rats. Tom snatched it up and tied it round one of the masts, tossing the other end into the river. Then, taking hold of the rope, he lifted himself over the railing that ran the full length of the deck, and began to lower himself down the side.

Dr Mobius's cabin was directly below him and a little to one side. Hanging in space with his arms out-stretched, his feet up against the side of the ship and his head hanging back, Tom was able to manoeuvre himself until he could look in through the window, into the cabin. He was about three metres below the deck and three metres above the frozen water of the Thames. If he let go of the rope he knew that he would fall right through the ice which still wasn't strong enough to support his weight. But it might be strong enough to trap him underneath the surface. Tom imagined himself in the chill, black water. He thought about Frank, the boy whose place he had taken. Would he have frozen before he drowned? Which would have killed him first?

Clinging on even tighter now, Tom looked into the cabin. The first thing he saw was that the monk wasn't a monk at all. He had taken off his robe and underneath he was dressed like a gentleman with a white collar, a black velvet cape, black stockings and black boots. The man had a beard and a moustache, both turning grey. His eyes were narrow and slightly too small for his head. His nose, long and hooked, was slightly too big for it. There was a long, tapering scar on the side of his cheek, shaped like a letter "J". From where Tom was hanging, he could also see a table, a chair, candles and a bed against the wall. But Dr Mobius himself was just out of sight.

"...the money? I haven't come right across London to leave without it."

It was the "monk" talking. With a thrill of excitement, Tom realized that he could hear every word the two men were saying. The cabin window might have had glass once but it had been broken or rotted away long ago. Tom eased himself closer, gently shifting his weight on his feet. He had to be careful. Move too quickly and he might find himself accidentally knocking on their wall.

"Of course I have the money," Mobius replied. A cloth bag appeared, thrown down on the table. It landed with a heavy clink. "But what I want to know, what you must tell me is..." His hand fell on the bag before the other man could take it. "...Do you have a result?"

"It's not easy, damn you," the man muttered. "I'm working on it. I'm sticking my neck out for you. Literally! I could lose my head for this!"

"But you're not doing it for me," Mobius purred. He lifted the bag again. "You're doing it for this. You're going to be very, very rich."

"If anyone finds out, I'm going to be very, very dead."

"They won't."

The man in black stood up and walked over to the window. Outside, Tom twisted away, afraid he was going to be discovered. For a nightmare moment he lost his footing and hung upside down, his neck twisted, and a sky of black ice filling his vision. But the man had turned round. Tom managed to loop the rope over his foot. He was still upside down. But he was safe.

"What about this new boy?" the man asked. "Who is he?"

"He's nobody. Nothing. A creature I picked out of the gutter." Mobius purred quietly and Tom could imagine him stroking his curling moustache.

"He doesn't know?"

"Of course not. He'll play his part and then we'll be rid of him. But we were talking about you, Sir Richard. When will I have a result?"

"Tomorrow. Maybe the day after. They're meeting soon..."

"You can take half the money now. Half later. And don't disappoint me, Sir Richard." There was a brief pause and Dr Mobius moved closer. Tom could just make out the side of his face and part of his body. One eye gleamed in the candlelight. "I have far-reaching friends. You may hide from me but not from them..."

Tom sensed that the interview was coming to an end and quickly pulled himself back up the side of the ship. He thought of the rope, stretching out across the deck. He couldn't risk Dr Mobius or the man he had called Sir Richard finding it.

There was nobody in sight on the deck. Tom climbed over the railing and untied the rope. He was just straightening up when a hand fell on his shoulder. Tom froze, then turned softly. Florian was standing over him. For a moment neither of them spoke. Tom wondered if the other boy was going to raise the alarm. He must have seen what Tom had been doing. He must know that Tom had been eavesdropping.

But then Florian began to speak, the words tumbling out as a whisper on a frosting cloud of breath. Tom couldn't understand what he was saying. The words made no sense. At last Florian stopped, but then he grabbed hold of Tom's sleeve. "Tom," he said. "I like you. But you have to go. Don't you see? You're in terrible danger. You must get off this ship. Leave London. Go as far away as you can..."

A door banged open. Mobius was showing the "monk" back to the shore. Florian turned and fled the other way. Tom stepped into the shadows, his mind whirling.

He had barely understood a word of what Florian had said. And it wasn't just because Tom had been taken by surprise or because all the blood had rushed to his head when he was upside down. No. It was only now that he realized. Florian had spoken to him for a minute, maybe for longer. But whatever language he had been speaking, it certainly wasn't English.

THIN ICE

There were no rehearsals on Christmas Day. Tom asked if he could leave the ship and was pleasantly surprised when Dr Mobius said yes. In fact, Mobius seemed quite keen for him to take a day's holiday.

Tom was glad to get back on to dry land. He walked for twenty minutes – it was easy to find his way. All he had to do was follow the river back down to London Bridge. Soon he was recognizing familiar landmarks. And it was just before midday when he found himself in front of the shoe shop over which Moll Cutpurse lived.

He was about to call up to her when Moll came out. She stopped and stared at him and, although she did her best to hide it, Tom knew that she was pleased to see him.

"So you decided to come back," she scowled.

"You did say I could look in on Christmas

Day," Tom replied.

Moll softened. "Oh yes. Happy Christmas." She ran her eye over him. "Well, you haven't been starving, I can see that," she said. "So does that mean you're an actor now?"

"Yes. I got a job!"

"Tried on the dress yet?" She smiled. "You'll look nice in make-up. In fact you'll probably make a much better girl than me." Somewhere in the distance a church clock chimed the hour. It was eleven o'clock. "I was just on my way to a Christmas dinner," Moll continued. "You're not invited, but since everyone there's going to be a crook anyway, I don't suppose they'd mind if you joined in."

Moll headed back through Southwark and past the great bull-baiting ring at Bankside. The other side of the river was heavily built up but on this side the buildings suddenly stopped, giving way first to gardens and then to open fields. The snow had fallen thicker here. To the south, everything was white with only a few cattle standing out against the landscape. Ahead of them, a single inn stood at the edge of a clump of trees. Moll went up to the door and knocked. The door opened a crack and a pair of dark eyes gazed suspiciously out.

"Moll!" a voice exclaimed.

The door opened fully and Moll and Tom went in.

It was a small inn but it was packed with

111

about twenty or thirty people sitting at a long table, chattering among themselves. As soon as they saw Moll and Tom, they bustled about making a space at the table so that the two new arrivals could sit down.

"Let me introduce you," Moll said to Tom. "That's Black Bob." She pointed at a man who was actually rather pale. "He's a highwayman. And so is One-eyed Jack..." She pointed to a second man. "...Snatcher Sam and old Shag-bag, there at the end of the table. Dick the Dealer there is a card sharp." She nodded at a man with a little pointy moustache and the man waved back, a pack of cards suddenly appearing from nowhere in his empty hand. "Over there are the Bird Brothers."

"London's finest burglars," the brothers – two plump men in identical green doublets – chorused in unison.

And then Tom remembered what Moll had said. "They're all crooks..." She had been speaking literally. *Everyone* at the inn was a thief of one sort or another. There were more pickpockets, several confidence tricksters, a passport forger, two hookers, two curbers and two divers. Tom wasn't sure what all these actually did, but they certainly looked very villainous with squinting eyes and wide, toothless smiles. It felt a bit strange to be the only person in the room who hadn't committed some sort of crime but then the food arrived and he soon found himself joining in the party with all his doubts forgotten.

It was a wonderful Christmas feast. There was a peacock pie, a goose and a pair of ducks. A whole boar's head arrived, chewing on an apple and even managing to look fairly cheerful considering it was being served up on a wooden plate. When that was all gone there was a pudding – a model of the Tower of London made entirely out of marzipan – which was carried into the room to cheers and applause. Finally there were hot chestnuts and more mulled ale and then someone brought out a fiddle and everyone began to sing though, unfortunately, not the same song.

Nobody had minded Tom being there and during the meal the card sharp had shown him how to strip out an ace and one of the confidence tricksters had tried to sell him London Bridge. But he had spent most of the time telling Moll about the Garden Players. He also told her about some of the mysteries of the past few days – the man with the scar who had come to the ship, Florian's warning and the strange marks on the arms of Dr Mobius and the actor called Ferdinand. Moll had made no comment on any of this but her eyes narrowed and as the meal went on she became quiet and thoughtful.

Outside, the sun was beginning to set and Tom considered that it was time to go. He got up and slipped out of the door. Moll came with him and the two of them stood for a minute in the dying light.

"Thank you, Moll," Tom said. He suddenly felt guilty. "I've got no money," he added. "How can I pay for my food?"

"I'll pay your share," Moll said. "You can pay me back when you're a famous actor."

They shook hands. Tom was about to leave but Moll stopped him. "The Garden Players..." she said, suddenly.

"What about them?"

"Nothing about them sounds quite right. A comedy that isn't funny. Dr Mobius. The way they just hired you without even hearing you read." She scowled. "When that boy, Florian, spoke to you, you said he was talking in a foreign language. You don't know what language it was?"

Tom shook his head. "All I know is, it wasn't English."

"Could it have been French? Or Dutch?"

"I don't know, Moll."

"No. You wouldn't." Moll sighed. Inside the tavern, there was a peal of laughter and clapping from the rest of the assembly. "I've got to go back in," Moll said. "But remember, Tom, if you get into any trouble, you only have to ask for me by name. Ask anyone – a beggar, a street-boy, a porter, a water-carrier. Just tell them to fetch Moll Cutpurse. They'll know

114

where to find me."

"I'm not in trouble…" Tom began.

"Not yet. But you might be." Moll shook her head, then turned round and went back into the inn.

Tom walked away. "I'm not in trouble," he had said. But he hadn't even taken ten paces and he was. Someone stepped out from behind a tree. The blade of a knife flashed in what was left of the fading light. A hand reached out and grabbed him roughly by the shirt, twisting him round.

"Good afternoon, Tom-Tom," Gamaliel Ratsey said in a soft, sing-song voice. "I thought I might find you here."

"Ratsey…!"

"My dear fellow! You don't know how glad I am to see you." Ratsey touched the point of the knife against Tom's neck. "Happy Christmas, by the way."

"How did you find me?"

"Oh, I heard that you and Moll – what's her name? – Cut-throat had teamed up together, so I've been keeping an eye on her. She led me here and I've been waiting ever since." He shivered. "Jolly cold, Tom-Tom. Deadly cold, you might say."

"What do you want with me?"

"I would have thought it was obvious. I must say, you rather let us down running off like that. The Slopes were very disappointed."

"I'm not going back to Framlingham!"

Ratsey smiled and waved the point of his dagger in a circle around Tom's head. "You're not going anywhere," he said.

"You're going to kill me!"

"It does rather look as if I'm going to have to," Ratsey agreed. "The thing is, you see, you know too much about me."

"I won't tell on you, Ratsey," Tom pleaded. "I've got a new life now, in London. I'm an actor. You can forget about me." He took a step back, trying to buy time, desperately searching for the right words. He had always been afraid of Ratsey and knew him for the killer that he was. But he wondered if there wasn't some way he could appeal to him. Surely there had to be some good in the man? "You can't just kill me in cold blood," he went on. "You're not like that..."

"But I am." Ratsey sighed, and for a moment he looked genuinely sad.

"No! You were a soldier. Captain Ratsey! You told me yourself. You fought for the Queen!"

"And what did the Queen ever do for me?" His eyes blazed. "Oh yes, I was once like you, Tom-Tom. A nice boy. A good boy. Fighting for the Queen to save the country. But when the fighting was over and the war was won, what happened? They gave me nothing! No pension. No reward. I was abandoned, left to starve, all on my own…"

"You had parents…"

"I'd run away from home. They didn't want to know me. There was no one to look after poor old Ratsey so I had to learn to look after myself. And that's what I'm doing now, Tom-Tom. I like you. Yes, I do. But, you see, you know too much. And maybe, one day, you'll whisper a few words … just by accident. Maybe in your sleep! I can't let that happen. I can't take the risk."

It was no good. Tom glanced left and right. They were standing in an open field, underneath a tree. Thick snow lay all around them and in the branches above. There was nobody in sight. Ratsey had led him away from the inn and Tom knew that even if he did call for help, he would be dead long before anyone arrived. Suddenly he felt very cold. Despite his new boots, the snow was reaching up to his ankles, penetrating his bones. The wind blew and a trickle of snow fell out of the tree and on to his neck.

The snow…

"So let's get this over with," Ratsey said. "I'm sorry, Tom. I hope you understand – it's nothing personal."

"Wait a minute, Ratsey!" Tom brought his hands together as if to plead for mercy. He was hoping he *had* learned something about acting in the last few days. "You can't kill me.

I'm only a child!"

"It's never stopped me before…"

"But I'm unarmed…" Now Tom turned his palms upwards. "Look! I don't have a weapon…" Slowly, Tom raised his arms.

"Most of the people I kill don't have weapons," Ratsey said, reasonably. "It makes it a lot easier." His fingers tightened on the knife. "Now stop all this nonsense, Tom-Tom. Time's up!"

Tom's hands were now over his head. There was a branch directly above him. His hands closed over it and with all his strength he pulled down.

A great clump of snow fell out of the tree, both on to Tom and on to Ratsey in front of him. Tom had been ready for it. Ratsey hadn't. Ratsey cursed, momentarily blinded. At the same moment, Tom turned and ran.

He was only seconds ahead of Ratsey. The highwayman had recovered fast and scooping the snow out of his eyes had launched himself after Tom. It was a strange, soundless pursuit. They were almost running in slow motion as their feet came down in the thick snow and even the sound of Tom's rasping breath was smothered by the frozen air.

Tom had no idea where he was going but realized – when it was too late – that he had managed to curve away from the inn where he might have found help. As he stumbled through the snow, almost slipping, scrabbling forward, he caught sight of a group of people, weaving slowly down a lane. Should he make for them? No. It was hopeless. They were probably half-drunk and before he could even begin to explain what was happening, Ratsey would have cut his throat.

"Tom...!"

He must have slowed down. Ratsey had almost caught up with him. The knife flashed through the air and Tom cried out as the very tip of it caught him on the shoulders, slicing through his shirt and drawing a line across his skin. The pain and the shock of it propelled him forward. Ratsey stumbled and almost lost his balance. Tom surged ahead.

He reached a row of houses, found an alleyway and ran through it. But it was then that he made his fatal mistake. Even as he ran, he looked back. His legs carried him the next ten metres before he knew what he had done and by the time he saw where he was it was too late.

He was near Bankside. He had entered a long, wooden jetty, stretching out into the River Thames. Unfortunately, the jetty only continued for another twenty metres and stopped. It was a passage to nowhere and before Tom could double back and regain dry land, Ratsey had reached the other end, blocking it.

The man and the boy stopped and stood

there, gazing at each other. Ratsey was breathing heavily. His dark hair had flopped across his face and he threw his head back to clear it. His eyes, when they were revealed, were alight with pleasure.

"You're a fast mover, Tom-Tom," he panted.

"Leave me alone, Ratsey…" Tom took two paces back. Two paces closer to the end of the jetty and the River Thames.

Ratsey lifted the knife and took another step. The jetty creaked underneath him.

"Tom, Tom, the piper's son…" Ratsey had begun to sing. "Cannot hide and he cannot run."

Tom had reached the end of the jetty. A wooden ladder led down to the Thames but there were no boats. Ratsey was getting closer. And then, in an instant, Tom knew what he had to do. Without taking his eyes off Ratsey he grabbed hold of the ladder and lowered himself down … not on to water. On to ice.

Ratsey stared for a moment, then darted forward. But he was already too late. Tom had backed away, wobbling uncertainly, but still standing upright on the ice. "Come back!" Ratsey squealed. His eyes flared and, slipping the knife between his teeth, he turned and launched himself down the ladder. But his feet had barely touched the ice before there was a sharp crack and with a shuddering scream he disappeared into a gaping hole that had suddenly appeared beneath him. If he hadn't been holding on to the ladder he would have been sucked into the black, freezing water. As it was, he barely had the strength to pull himself out and by the time he was back on top of the jetty, his teeth were rattling with cold.

"T...T...T... Tom!" he tried to call out. Tom was standing only a few metres away but now they could have been a world apart. "C...C... Come back!" Ratsey grabbed hold of himself as if trying to squeeze out the icy water. He no longer had the knife. He must have dropped it when he plunged into the river. "The ice! It won't hold your weight!"

"No thanks!" Tom slid backwards, not daring to lift his feet off the ice. He could feel it straining under his weight. Nobody else had tried to cross the Thames yet. It had been cold, but not cold enough. The ice was thin. In places it was almost transparent with the water oozing blackly through. But Tom was certain about one thing. He would sooner disappear through the ice and drown than go back to the jetty and face Ratsey again.

He kept walking. He didn't need to look back at Ratsey. He was a boy, small and underweight, and the ice was only just supporting him. Ratsey, as he had already proved, had no chance. Tom turned round and cried out as the ice gave away beneath him. One of his feet shot through into the water which closed around his ankle, instantly sucking out all feeling. Tom twisted sideways. Fortunately the ice was stronger here. With his foot dripping, he fought for balance and found it. For a moment he stood in the middle of the river, wondering which way to go, wondering if he could even find the courage to move.

Hunching his shoulders against the wind whipping up the river from Westminster, Tom continued across. It was much colder than he had thought. Out in the open, with nothing to protect him, his whole body was quickly growing numb. It was also much further than he would have liked. After ten minutes on the ice he wasn't even half way to the other side. A fist of loose snow punched into his face, forcing him to close his eyes. When he looked back, he could no longer see Ratsey. The highwayman must have given him up for lost.

He pressed on. The ice groaned and creaked but gradually the buildings on the other side of the river loomed up ahead of him, almost invisible in the darkness. Another wooden jetty reached out, water lapping at its legs. He took another step. The ice cracked. He yelled out and toppled forward, his arms flying out. Somehow his hands caught hold of wood. One leg disappeared into the water, soaking and freezing him all the way up to the thigh. But then he was out, pulling himself up on to the jetty. Behind him, shards of ice closed over the hole he had just made. More snow fell.

But he'd made it. He was safe.

It was night-time before Tom got back to the ship where the Garden Players were housed. It had taken him two hours to get there, partly because he was cold and exhausted, partly because he had been afraid of bumping into Ratsey. Although it was Christmas Day, the night watchmen were still out. Once he glimpsed a figure carrying a lantern and with a staff resting on his shoulder and he heard the familiar cry: *eight o'clock, look well to your locks, your fire and your light. God give you goodnight.*

The night still held one final surprise.

Tom had just got back to Bermondsey and was approaching the ship when he saw a man coming down the gangplank. The man came close to him and although he didn't see Tom, Tom recognized him by the monk's hood and robe he was wearing. It was the man with the scar, the one that Dr Mobius had called Sir Richard. The man hurried off into the night. Tom waited until he had gone, then walked over to the gangplank and went up on to the ship.

He had hoped to make it to the cabin without being seen, but he had barely moved before a door opened and Dr Mobius appeared, climbing up from below.

"Tom...?" Dr Mobius had a glass of wine in one hand, a pipe in the other. His cabin was lit by the soft yellow glow of a candle. He stepped out on to the deck.

"I have some good news for you!" Mobius stretched out a hand, his rings glinting in the candlelight. He laid it gently on Tom's head, stroking his hair. "We are going to perform *The Devil and his Boy* in three days' time."

"That's wonderful," Tom said.

"It is better than you think, my dear friend. We have been greatly honoured. Yes, indeed, it is an honour. The performance is to take place in the Palace of Whitehall."

"A palace?" Tom's mind was beginning to spin, but there was more to come.

"Yes, Tom." His lips curled in a slow smile and something brighter than candlelight gleamed in his eyes. "In Whitehall Palace. And we'll be performing in front of the Queen."

FIRST NIGHT NERVES

The next three days were a whirlwind of activity. There were still lines to be learned, movements to be discussed, fights to be choreographed and costumes to be sewn. And then there were the props and scenery. Like most plays, *The Devil and his Boy* didn't need much scenery – the audience was expected to imagine it. But there were a lot of props and it was one of these that led to a strange and unpleasant incident.

The prop was a pitchfork.

Tom was rehearsing on the deck in the cold morning sunlight. The entire cast was there, some of them acting, the rest sewing or painting. Florian, he noticed, was looking very downcast. In fact, the older boy had barely spoken a word to him since the night of the warning. However, he noticed Florian glance upwards sharply as Dr Mobius appeared from his cabin, carrying two pitchforks.

"This is for you, Tom," Dr Mobius said, handing him one. "When you disguise yourself as a devil, this is what you must carry. Please handle it with great care."

The pitchfork was about two metres long and taking it, Tom was surprised by its weight. Examining it, he soon knew why it was so heavy. The actual prongs themselves were only wood but the length of the pitchfork was a hollow metal tube – if it hadn't been for the prongs, glued to the top, Tom would have been able to look right through it. There was one other slightly strange thing. At the end of the tube, on the inside, some sort of line had been cut. Tom ran his thumb over it, feeling the sharp metal edge pressing into his flesh. Obviously the metal tube had been used for something before it had been turned into a fork. But why hadn't Dr Mobius used a broom handle or even a roll of paper? It would have been lighter and easier to handle.

And it was while they were running around the deck, that Tom dropped his. The pitchfork fell down. The wooden forks snapped off and the metal tube began to roll along the deck.

Everyone froze. The tube was heading towards the very edge of the ship. There were no railings there. There was nothing between it and the river. And then Florian reacted. Acting as if his life depended on it, he threw himself full-length on to the deck. His outstretched hand caught the tube centimetres away from the edge. He stood up, holding it.

Dr Mobius had watched all this with wide eyes. Tom could see the relief in his eyes as Florian lifted the tube, but in seconds relief had been replaced with fury. His whole face seemed to change. His skin grew darker, the veins standing out on his bald head. His mouth drew back in a snarl and the next thing Tom knew his hand had struck out, crashing into the side of Tom's face and throwing him sprawling on to the deck. With his head spinning, he tried to stand up but Dr Mobius was already there, looming over him.

"You idiot!" Dr Mobius shouted. "You fool! I told you to be careful and you almost lost it!"

"It's only a metal tube!" Tom protested.

"What?" Dr Mobius drew back his foot and Tom was sure he was going to kick him where he lay. But then Florian sprang forward.

"It was an accident," he said. "You don't have to hurt him!"

Dr Mobius stared at his nephew with murder in his eyes. For his part, Florian held his ground, the rod still in his hand.

Slowly, Dr Mobius recovered. He looked down. Tom was still on his knees. There was a trickle of blood coming from the side of his mouth. Dr Mobius drew a hand over his eyes as if trying to wipe away the memory of what had just occurred.

"You must forgive me," he said. "That was ... unforgivable of me." He whipped out his handkerchief and offered it to Tom. Tom didn't take it. "You see," he went on, "to play in front of the Queen! It is a considerable honour. And of course ... I am nervous. We are all nervous. And this..." He gestured at the metal tube, then at Tom. "It was first night nerves. I apologize to you. It won't happen again." He took the metal rod from Florian and stepped back. "We shall all take a rest," he exclaimed to the watching actors. "We will start again after lunch."

The actors dispersed. Tom looked for Florian but the other boy had already turned away and gone downstairs. Suddenly resolved, Tom got up and followed him.

He found Florian in the costumes room, at work on the dress that he himself would wear. Tom paused in the doorway. He caught sight of himself in a piece of broken mirror leaning against the wall. There was still a little blood beside his mouth and he wiped it away with his sleeve.

"Thank you," he said.

"That's all right." Florian didn't look up from his work.

"Florian..." Tom moved further into the room. "The other night ... last week. You told me I should get off the ship. You said that I was in danger. What did you mean?"

The other boy turned his head away. The dress he was working on was bunched up in his hands. Tom could almost feel him struggling with himself. But then another of the actors appeared at the door and looked in. "Lunch is ready," he said and went on his way.

Maybe Florian had been about to tell Tom something but the moment had been interrupted and now the spell was broken. "I didn't mean anything," he said. "I shouldn't have said it. Just forget it."

He got up and, brushing past Tom, quickly left the room.

The opening performance of the first night drew closer and closer. They ran through the play once, then again, this time, with costumes as well as props. Florian had been transformed into a girl with a flowing dress, make-up and a wig. Watching him, Tom remembered his meeting with Will Shakespeare and wondered if he could have acted as a girl at the Rose. In his heart, he knew he could. He also knew – although it made him sad – that he would much rather be acting in Shakespeare's new play than in *The Devil and his Boy*.

The last morning came and went. Everyone knew their lines. Francis and Frances, the musicians, knew their tunes. They performed the play one last time, and this time Dr Mobius loaded the muskets so that, as he and Tom were chased off the stage (this was the last scene of the play), there were loud explosions and puffs of smoke behind them.

Dr Mobius was pleased with the effect. "It will give Her Majesty much pleasure. The explosions and the alarms." He rolled his moustache between two fingers. "Everyone enjoys that in a play. The last act has to be the best!"

That afternoon, they left the boat. A horse and cart had arrived and all the props, costumes, stage furniture and scripts were carried across in trunks and loaded up in the back. Tom was already feeling dry-mouthed and wondered what he would be like when they arrived at Whitehall Palace.

When everything had been loaded, he and Florian climbed into the back. There was room for the two boys and for Dr Mobius at the front of the cart, but everyone else would have to walk. They stood waiting in the cold for a few minutes. Dr Mobius was the last to leave the ship. He looked briefly in the back of the cart.

"Are you ready?" he asked.

"Yes, Dr Mobius."

"Then onward ... to glory!"

Dr Mobius climbed into the front of the cart

and a moment later they felt a jolt as it moved off. Tom glanced back. And it was then that he saw something moving on the deck. It was smoke. It was coming up from below, creeping over the deck and curling round the masts. At first he thought he must be mistaken but suddenly a tongue of flame shot out, licked at part of the old rigging and suddenly the whole boat was ablaze.

Tom cried out but Florian leaned over and stopped him. "It's all right, Tom," he said. "We're finished here. We won't be going back."

The cart rumbled onward. The entire boat was ablaze now, huge flames reaching up to the very top of the masts. As damp as the ship was, the fire seemed to fall on it like a hungry animal, tearing into it, consuming it utterly. The wood cracked and splintered. One of the masts shivered and fell. The flames leapt up. The ice on the river, glowing red now, began to move, pulling away from the doomed vessel. Slowly the old ship folded in on itself.

And then the cart turned a corner and Tom saw no more.

Whitehall Palace was quite unlike anything Tom had dreamed of. He had imagined a single building but as the cart passed the great monument at Charing Cross and trundled underneath the arches of the Holbein Gate, he

131

realized that it was an entire town in its own right. There were soaring chapels and tall, solid towers; elegant stables and neat, compact houses. The entire complex was set in gardens and orchards, spread out on the northern bank of the Thames. Tom found it hard to believe that only a few days before he had been close by, fighting for his life on the fragile ice.

They were stopped by a soldier dressed in a red and black tunic with a sword at his waist and an odd weapon – part spear and part axe – on his shoulder. Sitting at the front of the cart, Dr Mobius produced a letter and handed it to him and the soldier directed them to a large building that was being guarded by two more similarly dressed men. The cart rolled across the last few metres and Tom got down. The two men seemed to take no notice of him. Passing between them, Tom went in – and found himself in the Banqueting Hall where the play was to be performed.

It was a huge space, at least a hundred metres long, held up by slim wooden pillars garlanded with dried flowers and fruit. The walls seemed to be solid stone but looking more closely, Tom was thrilled to realize that the whole building was a trick. The walls were actually made of canvas. What he was standing in was nothing more than a gigantic tent. But what a tent! The ceiling had been painted as if it were the sky – at one end there were silver stars and a moon, at the other a golden sun, shooting out its beams. At least three hundred glass lamps hung inside and wreaths of holly and ivy had been placed everywhere.

A stage had been constructed at one end of the Banqueting Hall. It stood against a screen which the actors could hide behind when they needed to change or were waiting to come on. There were a number of chairs at the other end, one of them larger than the rest and richly padded with velvet and cushions. Tom didn't need to ask who would be sitting here.

Dr Mobius had already started carrying in the costumes and props. Tom wondered if he ought to help but before he could move there was the sound of stamping feet and a dozen soldiers suddenly marched in, forming a line on either side of the entrance. There was a brief pause and then three more men came in, these ones wearing brilliantly coloured slashed doublets and caps, tight stockings and highly polished shoes.

Dr Mobius stopped what he was doing and bowed low. The actors did the same. Tom hesitated for a moment then remembered himself and bowed as well. The man standing in the middle – he also had some sort of chain of office round his neck and carried a white staff – gestured at Dr Mobius, who straightened up.

"My name is Edmund Tilney," he said. "I am Master in the Office of the Revels. You are..." He creased his brow and glanced at the younger man on his left.

"The Garden Players," the man said.

"Quite. And the name of the play you are to perform?"

"*The Devil and his Boy*," Dr Mobius told him.

"Oh yes." The Master of the Revels frowned. "Not an entirely suitable title, I feel," he snapped. "But Sir Richard says he found it most enjoyable."

At the mention of Sir Richard, Tom glanced up. He had barely noticed the third man when he came in but now he realized that it was indeed the same "Sir Richard" who had come – twice – to the boat. There were the narrow eyes and slightly hooked nose. And there – impossible to miss – was the scar, cut on the side of his cheek, shaped like a J.

But even as he stood there uncomfortably with his back bent and his neck craning up, Tom's mind began to race. As far as he knew, *The Devil and his Boy* had never been performed before. Certainly all the actors had had to learn it from scratch. So how could Sir Richard claim to have seen it?

And why had Sir Richard come to the boat, not only at night but in disguise? He remembered seeing Dr Mobius give him a bag full of coins. What had the money been for?

And, most strangely of all, why were Dr

Mobius and Sir Richard pretending they didn't know each other? It wasn't just that they hadn't greeted each other. They weren't even looking each other in the eye.

What exactly was going on?

"All right," Tilney was saying. "The play will begin at eight o'clock, after Her Majesty has finished dinner. There are certain rules which you would be wise to obey." He cast his eyes over the entire company. "None of you are to look at Her Majesty. If she enjoys the play, she may come and speak to you afterwards. If she doesn't, I can assure you that she's the *last* person you'd want to speak to. Don't try to speak to *her*. You may find it easier just to imagine she isn't here."

He paused for breath. From the way he spoke, Tom imagined that he had done this many times before.

"Now, we have to consider the content of this play. I understand it's a comedy. I hope it's got good jokes."

"The very finest, my lord," Dr Mobius said, bowing again.

"Good. Her Majesty enjoys a laugh. If you don't hear her laughing, I suggest you finish it as quickly as you can. Leave out Acts Three and Four if you have to." He turned to Sir Richard. "There's nothing vulgar in it, is there?" he asked.

"No, my lord," Sir Richard replied.

"Nothing offensive, sacrilegious, unpatriotic or treasonable? I have to remind you that the Bishop of Winchester is in tonight, and you know how touchy he gets. The devil in this play. We're not talking about Satan, I hope?"

"It's not the real devil, my lord," Dr Mobius said.

"Good. Good. Good... Now, let me see." He gestured at Sir Richard. "Sir Richard here is the Clerk Comptroller. If all goes well he'll pay you ten pounds, once the play is finished. If Her Majesty walks out half-way, it'll be five pounds. Do you understand?"

Everyone who had stopped bowing bowed again.

"Now, there's one last thing," Tilney said. "Sir Richard informs me that you fire muskets in the last act."

"They are fake muskets," Dr Mobius exclaimed. "I can assure my lord that Her Majesty will be entertained and not alarmed..."

"Yes! Yes! Yes!" Tilney interrupted. "All your props and luggage will be searched by the Gentlemen Pensioners before she arrives." He gestured at the men in red. "They'll also search every one of you, too. But I think I'd better take a look at these muskets of yours myself."

Dr Mobius nodded and two of the actors carried forward the trunk that contained the two muskets. They opened it and handed the weapons to Tilney who glanced at them briefly. "As you will see, my lord," Mobius explained, "the barrels of the guns are fashioned from wood. They are also solid. No ball could pass through them. The only part of the weapon that is authentic is the firing mechanism. We require this to make the ... small explosions – which, I can assure, my lord, will add a delightful frisson to Her Majesty's evening."

Tilney nodded and set the weapons down. "Very good." He nodded at the Gentlemen Pensioners. "Make sure they're all thoroughly searched."

It took over an hour to search everyone and everything. The Gentlemen Pensioners were the Queen's personal bodyguard and it was their job to ensure that nothing remotely dangerous came anywhere near her. Even a small knife that Mobius used to sharpen his quill was removed. The muskets were examined again and set down on a table along with the pitchforks, the devil horns and all the other bits and pieces from the play. Only when they were completely satisfied did the Gentlemen Pensioners leave and even then two of them remained behind to guard the door and make sure that nobody else tried to enter.

For the next three hours, Tom helped get the stage ready, constructing the scenery, setting out the furniture and ensuring that everything was in its right place. All the props and costumes had to be carried behind the screen and arranged out-of-sight. The instruments had to be tuned. And finally there were hurried consultations with the actors whispering their lines to each other, making sure there was nothing they had forgotten. During all this, Tom noticed, Florian didn't say a word. Once Tom tried to speak to him but the other boy hurriedly broke away as if he were afraid of catching – or giving Tom – the plague.

At last everything was ready. Someone had brought the players some bread, some cold meat and wine, but everyone was too nervous to eat. Dr Mobius, however, poured himself a cup of wine and held it up in a toast.

"Today," he said, "is the day that we make history." All the actors were gathered around listening. They seemed to share the same, strange gleam in their eyes. Only Florian looked sick and kept his head down. "The 28th December 1593," Dr Mobius went on, "It is a day that no one in England will forget. It is a day that will belong to the *Garduna*." He blinked and then turned to Tom with a smile. "I mean, of course, the Garden Players." He lifted his cup. "I drink to you, my friends. To the sacrifice we make for our country. May God bless all of us in this great endeavour. Glory … and death!"

It seemed a very strange speech to be making

just before a play, and a comedy at that. But the actors (apart from Florian) had all whispered a fervent "amen" and Tom joined them, not wishing to be left out. It still puzzled him though and he was about to ask Dr Mobius what he had meant when there was a trumpet fanfare and a sudden murmur of voices on the other side of the screen.

At once the room began to fill up. Tom was forbidden to look round the screen but he heard men and women talking, the clattering of shoes, the scrape of chairs being moved and an occasional burst of laughter. Next to him, Francis and Frances began to give their instruments a final tuning.

And then, as suddenly as it had started, the noise stopped. There was a second fanfare and everyone in the room stood up. Tom still couldn't see anything but he knew what had happened.

The Queen had arrived.

The lights dimmed as most of the candles were blown out.

The audience took their places.

And the play began.

THE DEVIL AND HIS BOY

The play began with a prologue, delivered by
Dr Mobius himself. Tom had heard it twenty
or more times but listening to it now from
behind the screen, he barely understood a
word of it. It was as if there were a wind rushing through his ears. He couldn't hear anything. His mouth was dry. There was no
feeling in his arms or legs.

He was, he realized, terrified. He was about
to go on the stage in front of Queen Elizabeth
and her court. He wondered if his legs would
be able to move when his cue came. Not for
the first time, he wished he had never left
Framlingham. Even life with the Slopes had
been better than this.

Act One, Scene One began. Lucio had
arrived in Venice. He had no money and
nowhere to stay for the night. He called for his
servant.

140

"Antonio! What ho? Antonio...!"

Tom stepped through the screen and on to the stage.

And the strange thing was, he left all his fear behind him. He had never felt such a transformation. It was as if he had stepped out of water on to dry land. Suddenly he was confident. He knew his lines. He knew what to do. It might have been Tom who had stood fearful and quivering behind the screen. But it was Antonio, servant of Lucio who now began to talk, poking fun at his master and finally racing round the stage as he tried to escape a beating.

Tom didn't dare look into the shadows beyond the stage but he could tell that the audience was enjoying the play. They had been silent throughout the prologue and the opening scene but Tom's entrance had cheered them up. They laughed quite a few times and when the scene ended they clapped.

Tom hurried off the stage. He wondered if the Queen herself had clapped with them. The Queen of England, applauding him! But he didn't have time to think about it. The props were laid out on a table behind a fake wall – built for Act Five – and he hurried over and picked up the two pitchforks.

He was half-way back to the stage before he knew something was wrong and even then he wasn't sure what it was. At first he thought he had forgotten something. He had the pitch-forks, the rope, the horns. What else was there? On the stage, Dr Mobius was coming to the end of another soliloquoy and Tom knew he had only moments before he had to go back on. He was wearing horns. He had put on his tail.

And then he understood what it was. The pitchforks were much too light. Being careful not to drop them, Tom turned them over in his hands and examined them. He quickly saw what had happened. The forks at the top were the same but the long metal tubes had been replaced with lengths of wood. This made them much lighter to carry and easier to handle too. But Tom was surprised that Dr Mobius should have changed them at this late stage and that he should have done so without telling him.

"Here comes Antonio now!"

Caught up with the pitchforks, Tom had almost missed his cue. He hurried on to the stage, almost dropping them as he went and although Dr Mobius glared at him, this got another laugh from the audience. The rest of the scene was a nightmare. Tom twisted one of his lines so it came out all wrong and completely forgot another. But try as he might, he found it almost impossible to concentrate. Ever since he had joined the Garden Players all sorts of questions had been tapping at the window of his mind. He had tried to ignore them. But now, at the worst possible time, they had returned, louder and more insistent than ever.

Somehow he made it to the end of the scene but when he got backstage a furious Dr Mobius – looking more devilish than ever – marched up to him and grabbed him.

"What are you doing?" he demanded in a hoarse whisper. His eyes were bulging with the effort of not shouting and his make-up had begun to run.

"I'm sorry…" On the other side of the screen, Francis and Frances, the two musicians, were playing a duet.

Dr Mobius closed his eyes, forcing himself to regain control. "Remember what you are doing," he said. "Concentrate!" He glared at Tom, then withdrew into the shadows.

Tom took a deep breath, angry with himself. Dr Mobius was right. Whatever his doubts about the play, the Garden Players and everything to do with them, he couldn't worry about them now. And what was so important about the pitchforks anyway? Once they had been metal. Now they were wood.

The pitchfork rolling across the deck. Florian diving and catching it. Dr Mobius hitting him. "You idiot! You fool! You almost lost it!"

Tom shook his head, forcing himself to forget it. Behind the screen, the duet finished.

The next scene began.

There were no further mishaps. Tom made no more mistakes, and an hour later he left the stage knowing that he would not be needed now until the very end of Act Five. It was the interval.

With the actors safely hidden behind the screen, the doors were opened and the audience retired for refreshments in another part of the palace. Tom was exhausted. Performing had sucked all the energy out of him. The other actors seemed as tired as he was. They also looked nervous and this was surprising. The play was more than half over. The most difficult scenes were behind them. Why should they seem so nervous now?

Edmund Tilney, the Master of the Revels, had come backstage. The man with the scar came with him. Sir Richard seemed to have caught a cold. He was pale and sweating.

"Her Majesty will be returning for the second half," Tilney said.

"We are honoured." Dr Mobius bowed low.

"Yes. You are." Tilney coughed drily. "The play's too long and it's rather dull. I'd be grateful if you could speed up Acts Four and Five. However, Her Majesty likes the boy – and the one playing the girl. She also likes the music. I take it there is more music?"

"A great deal more," Dr Mobius assured him.

"Good." Tilney glanced at his Clerk Comptroller. "I must say, Sir Richard," he snapped, "this hasn't been one of your best recommendations."

He turned to leave but Dr Mobius stopped him. "Wait until the end of the performance before you pass judgement, my lord," he said. "I think I can promise you that it is a play that Her Majesty will not forget. Nor you either!"

Tilney raised his eyebrows at this but said nothing. He left the room, Sir Richard hurrying after him.

Dr Mobius and the other actors were sitting on benches, some lying on their backs with their eyes closed. Florian was on his own, gnawing at his fingernails and staring into space. It was very dark behind the stage. Tom was glad about that. The darkness helped him think.

Someone had changed the pitchforks. Why? Back on the ship, Dr Mobius had almost killed him when he had dropped one of them. But why had the pitchforks been made of metal in the first place – and why metal tubes?

Metal tubes. For some reason that made Tom think of something. But what? Tom buried his head in his hands and searched through his memory. A metal tube, pointing at him. Of course! He was back in the forest with Hawkins. He was looking at Ratsey's gun.

There were guns in Act Five of *The Devil*

and his Boy as well. Tom still hadn't solved the puzzle but suddenly he was filled with dread. The Master of the Revels had checked the muskets himself.

Tom remembered what Dr Mobius had said: *"The barrels of the guns are fashioned from wood."*

Moving slowly, trying to act as natural as possible, Tom went over to the artificial wall behind which the props were kept. He took one last look to make sure nobody was watching. Then he slipped behind the wall.

The muskets were lying in the right place, waiting for their appearance in Act Five. They looked exactly the same as they had earlier that afternoon when Tilney had examined them, but even as he reached for the nearest one, Tom knew it had changed. Sure enough, it was heavier. He turned it round. The barrel of the gun was no longer made of wood. Nor was it solid.

And in that moment, Tom knew everything.

It was very simple.

Dr Mobius was planning to kill the Queen! He was going to do it at the end of Act Five with muskets that, with the metal rods from the pitchforks screwed into place, were now *real* muskets. One shot for the Queen. One shot for the guard by the door. Maybe Dr Mobius and the Garden Players planned to fight their way out. But Tom had seen the fanatical light in Dr Mobius's eyes. He had a job to do. He wouldn't care what happened to him when it was over.

Gently, Tom lowered the musket back on to the table. What could he do?

He had to save the Queen – but that might be easier said than done. How could he even leave the backstage area without the others seeing? And if he did manage to slip away, where could he go? Who could he tell? Sir Richard was obviously a traitor. What about Edmund Tilney? But if he did speak out, would anyone believe him?

The problem was solved for him.

Tom hadn't heard anyone creeping round behind the wall but the next moment something cold and hard crashed into the back of his neck. His legs buckled under him. The darkness came rushing in. He tried to fight it. But then Dr Mobius hit him again and he was gone.

Tom woke up slowly with a pain in his head and a neck that felt as if it had been tied in a knot. He was lying underneath the table, his face pressed against the floor. He could taste straw and sawdust in his mouth. Even before he opened his eyes, he heard the play being performed in what seemed like the far distance. It took him a minute to make out the words and another minute to recall where they came from. Act Five, Scene Two. Just a few pages until Lucio and Antonio were chased out of Venice by soldiers armed with...

He remembered the muskets and crawled painfully out from under the table. The muskets weren't there. He looked over to the side of the screen and saw Frederick and Philip, two of the actors, dressed as soldiers and carrying the muskets, waiting for their cue. He knew what was going to happen. In about one minute's time, they would walk on to the stage. Nobody would even think of stopping them. They would raise their muskets, loaded and primed. There would be two explosions and the audience probably wouldn't even realize what had taken place. Until they saw the Queen's blood.

Tom had to stop them. But even now he didn't know what to do. Shout out a warning? It wouldn't work. The two actors would fire before the Queen had time to move. Throw himself at Frederick and Philip? No. Even assuming he could get anywhere near them, he couldn't take on two men at once.

These merry devils must be banished hence.
Go! Call the watch...!

Tom knew the lines. The shooting was about to begin. There was no time to call out a warning. No time to try and explain.

Before he knew what he was doing, he was running – round behind the screen and out on

148

to the stage. All the actors had their backs to him so none of them saw him as he broke into the light and kept on going. Tom just had time to glimpse Florian, turning his head towards him, his eyes widening, and next to him, Dr Mobius himself, his mouth half-open in mid-sentence. He had no real plan. All he knew was that he must put himself in front of the Queen, protect her with his own body if he had to. Only seconds remained before Mobius would fire the first shot. Even now he might be taking aim.

Tom had reached the front of the stage. Everything was a whirl. He tried to position himself, spreading his arms to give the Queen more cover. And it was then that his foot came down on a loose plank. The wood tilted and he lost his balance. With a great cry he pitched forward and, carried by his own momentum, plunged down on to the Queen herself.

Then things didn't so much happen as explode. Tom fell on top of the Queen, knocking her chair backwards and sending her flying. There was a gasp of disbelief from the surrounding courtiers, screams from the Maids of Honour. Tom just caught sight of the Queen's face, wide-eyed with shock. He was vaguely aware of black teeth and skin with too much make-up. To his horror, the Queen seemed to be wearing a wig which had come loose. He closed his eyes. The very fact that he was touching her was beyond belief. Actually to be lying on top of her, his body on hers, his hands around her throat ... it was enough to give an Archbishop a heart attack. He couldn't look. He didn't dare.

But even though it had all gone horribly wrong, he knew that he had succeeded in what he set out to do. His attack had taken Dr Mobius by surprise. Already the audience had closed in on the Queen. The Gentlemen Pensioners were running in from all sides to pull him off.

Tom didn't know if Dr Mobius had a musket now or not. But it didn't matter. He had no clear aim.

Dr Mobius did have a musket. He had snatched it from Frederick even as Tom ran past. Standing at the front of the stage, he waved it at the writhing, panicking mass that had been a courtly audience only seconds before. He caught sight of a stockinged leg, a jewelled foot and fired.

The sound of the explosion seemed huge and suddenly the hall was filled with smoke and the smell of gunpowder. But the shot had missed. One of the courtiers had been shot in the back of his leg. With blood spurting from the wound, he cried out and fell to the ground.

The gun-shot only added to the panic in the hall. Nobody quite knew where it had come from. All they knew was that one of the actors, the boy, had gone mad and thrown himself at the Queen and now somebody else had decided to join him. At least a dozen pairs of hands had grabbed Tom and he felt himself being ripped apart while, still underneath him, the Queen had brought up her fists and was vigorously punching him on the nose and the stomach.

But at least some of the courtiers had kept their heads. The boy on top of the Queen was an outrage. But now there was a musket somewhere in the room – and that was a deadly danger. Acting out of instinct, the courtiers had moved to surround the Queen, forming a human wall for her protection. At the same time, the Gentlemen Pensioners had formed a front line, making for the stage.

Dr Mobius knew he was finished. He grabbed the second musket and once again stared into the commotion. But now there was no sign of the Queen at all. With a loud oath, he fired again, as if he could aim through so much writhing flesh and blood and still, miraculously find his target. The second shot did get some way through. It hit Tom in the shoulder. He felt it slamming into his body, white hot and furious. It was like the sting of some terrible insect. Tom screamed. At the same time he felt himself being plucked away. He opened his eyes and caught one last sight of the Queen. It was as if she were being sucked into a tunnel in front of him. A fist hit him on the side of the face. Another hand tore at his hair. He was flung to the floor, his bones crashing into wood, and when he tried to move he found that he was pinned there, held down by at least five men.

Up on the stage, the actors were trying to fight their way out. But the two muskets, with their single shots gone, were useless now and they had no other weapons. It was all over very quickly. Only two of the actors – the two who had also played musical instruments – were killed. Later on it would be agreed that they had run on to the swords held up to stop them leaving, preferring to kill themselves rather than face imprisonment, torture and a more protracted death.

The Queen had been helped to her feet and disappeared with a swirl of silk. She was followed by bishops and courtiers, secret agents and councillors, already arguing amongst themselves, and by ladies-in-waiting who had turned into ladies-in-wailing as they sobbed in both terror and relief.

Someone rapped out an order and Tom was scraped off the floor and lifted out of a puddle of his own blood. He stood, swaying on his feet. A couple of men supported him. He could never have stood on his own. Somehow he managed to bring his eyes into focus and saw Sir Richard, standing at the edge of the crowd.

The Clerk Comptroller's face had gone completely white – all of it except for the scar which stood out, dark red and throbbing. His eyes were filled with terror.

But then another man, someone Tom had never seen before pushed his way forward. This man was dressed in black and grey with a chain of office around his neck and a sword in his belt. The man had soft, green eyes. His face was long and thin. "Who are you?" he asked.

Tom tried to answer. He opened his mouth but nothing came out.

The man with green eyes looked at him more in puzzlement than in anger. "Why did you do it?" he asked.

"I didn't..." It took all Tom's strength to whisper the two words and even as he spoke them he knew it would be no good. Everyone in the room had seen what had happened. Nobody would believe him.

"Take him away!" the man said. "The others to the Tower for interrogation. This boy to Newgate. He has lain a hand on the most glorious person of Her Majesty. He has ... *attacked* her! Such sacrilege is unheard of and we must ensure that no one does hear of it. Hang him tomorrow at first light. We'll learn from the others the reason for what happened here."

"Wait..." Tom began.

153

But already he was being dragged backwards out of the Banqueting Hall. He felt the cold night air rushing over his shoulders and its touch brought fresh pain from the wound in his back. There was a cart and a horse already waiting and brutally, like a sack of potatoes, he was thrown into the back. Two guards climbed in with him. The horse was whipped forward.

Tom thought he was going to faint with the shock, the pain, the knowledge of what was to come. The night began to spin but before he let it take him, he forced his eyes open and looked out. They had just passed through the Holbein Gate. There were a few late-night revellers on the other side, making their way home with a servant – a link-boy – lighting their way. Tom lifted himself in the cart and before his two guards could stop him, called out, "Find Moll Cutpurse! Tell her it wasn't me! Tell her that Tom…!"

Then the guards reached him, grabbed him and pulled him down and Tom could say no more. Had the link-boy even heard him? Tom didn't know and he was too exhausted to care. He closed his eyes and drifted into sleep as the cart rattled on through the night.

ON THE SCAFFOLD

It was seven o'clock in the morning and Gamaliel Ratsey was enjoying a healthy breakfast of hot porridge, bread, honey and milk in the tavern where he had been staying since his arrival in London. The owners of the tavern had let him have his bed and breakfast at a special rate. In return, Ratsey had promised not to kill them.

He looked up. Someone was standing over him, watching him with soft, attentive eyes. Automatically, Ratsey's hand twitched for the hilt of his sword. Then he relaxed. It wasn't a man but a boy, and not a boy but a girl. He knew at once who it was.

"Moll Cut-throat!" he exclaimed. "This is a surprise."

"It's Cutpurse," Moll replied. "May I join you?"

"It looks like you already have." Ratsey

scooped up a mouthful of porridge. "Have you come to bring me the boy?"

"Not exactly." Moll gazed curiously at Ratsey as if trying to make him out. "I have something to tell you," she said.

"Go on." Ratsey gave her his best, choirboy smile

"Tom Falconer is in Newgate. He's going to be hanged at eleven o'clock this morning."

Ratsey chuckled. "Is he, indeed? How do you know?"

"I heard last night."

Quickly, Moll told Ratsey how she had been woken by the link-boy and how, at first light she had gone to Newgate Prison to find out what had taken place. Nobody had wanted to tell her anything but she had bribed one of the guards with sixpence and heard the complete story from him.

"Tom is accused of trying to kill the Queen," she told Ratsey now.

"That's ridiculous!"

"Of course it is. Tom would never try to kill anyone. All he wanted to do was act in a play. But these people he got involved with ... they called themselves the Garden Players, but I've been asking around and nobody has heard of them – and from what Tom told me they weren't English."

"Maybe they were French."

"Or Dutch. Or Spanish. It doesn't matter.

All that matters is that Tom can't have had anything to do with it. But he's going to hang in less than four hours if you and I don't do something."

"You and I?" Ratsey choked on his porridge. "You're mad! Why should I care if they hang the boy? They'll be doing me a favour."

"Is that your answer?"

"Yes. I always liked Tom. To be honest with you, I was never looking forward to murdering him. But what on earth makes you think I'd want to help him?"

This was the moment Moll had been dreading. She knew she'd taken a huge chance coming here. But she needed Ratsey's help and this was the only way. "I know who you are, Ratsey," she said. "But I also know who you used to be."

Ratsey's eyes narrowed. The smile faded from his lips. "What the devil are you talking about?" he asked.

"I'm talking about Captain Ratsey. The famous soldier who fought in the Irish campaigns and single-handedly captured the fort at Smerwick." She nodded gravely. "Oh yes, I've heard all the stories about you," she went on. "People talk about Sir Francis Drake and Sir Walter Raleigh. But you could have been a bigger hero than either of them."

"Could have been! Could have been! But that was then!" Ratsey threw down his spoon.

"That was a long time ago. Now I'm Ratsey the robber. Ratsey the killer. It's too late for me now."

"That's what I'm trying to tell you. This could be your last chance!" Moll reached out to take his arm but Ratsey pulled it away. "People like us, Ratsey – pickpockets and highwaymen. What sort of life do we have? Always afraid. Always on the run. Until one day they catch up with us and then..." Moll drew her hands to her throat. "But this is a chance to do one good thing. To be remembered as heroes. To make something of ourselves."

Ratsey fell silent. "So what are you suggesting, Moll Cut-price?" he demanded at length. "We just walk into Newgate and pull Tom out?"

"No. We go to Whitehall – to the Queen."

"What? Old Queeny!"

"Yes. We'll tell her she's made a mistake. We'll make her listen to us..."

"You think they'll even allow us in?"

"I know how to get us in, Ratsey. But I can't do it alone." Moll gripped his arm and this time he let her. "Doesn't Tom deserve a chance?" she said. "You said you liked him. Save his life and maybe you'll be saving your own. Think of what you were. Think of what you still can be."

Ratsey sighed. "My father always said I'd

come to no good," he said. "He said I'd end up on the wrong end of a rope."

"So prove him wrong."

Ratsey thought for a long minute. He stuck a finger in his porridge and stirred it, then licked the finger. The porridge was cold. He sighed again. Then, finally, he saluted. "All right. All right. Captain Ratsey reporting for duty," he muttered. "Now tell me. What's the plan?"

There were fourteen prisons in London but Newgate was the most feared. It was reserved for the very worst criminals and all of them arrived in the knowledge that they would not be staying long. Nine steps led to the way out. A rope and a trap-door. Tom, however, was about to set the record for the shortest stay of all. And although the guards argued about this, they were fairly sure that he would be the youngest person they had ever hanged.

Tom awoke in a small, square cell, lying on a thin layer of straw with a tattered blanket over his legs. A small, barred window – another square – looked out on to grey sky and little else. He was not alone. A short, round man was lying on a bench, his knees tucked into his ample stomach, snoring loudly. Tom sat up. His shoulder, where he had been shot, still hurt dreadfully and there was no movement at all in his right arm. He was filthy and his head ached.

The man on the bench grunted, sat up and rubbed his eyes. Tom barely glanced at him but the man gazed at Tom, shook his head, then... "My dear fellow!" he exclaimed. "It's John, is it not? No, it's not. It's Tim! No, it's not. It's Tom!" He smiled. "There have been so many boys. So many charming boys. I'm afraid I get a little hazy with names."

Now Tom recognized his cell-mate. The last time they had met, he had been interested in removing Tom's legs. The man was James Grimly. "What are you doing here?" Tom was so astonished that the words just tumbled out.

"A most serious misunderstanding with the authorities. They take a dim view, it would seem, of my ... adjustments. Quite why, I cannot say. I feel London will be a much less cheerful place without Grimly's boys. But there you are." He sighed. "One or two of my boys became rather ill," he admitted. "In fact, not to put too fine a point on it, they died. So now they've decided to adjust *me*." He ran a finger across his throat. "Permanently."

"They're going to hang me too," Tom said.

"My poor fellow! What did you do?"

Tom half-smiled. "I tried to kill the Queen."

"Good lord!" Grimly blinked rapidly. "I have to say, Tom, I'm quite shocked. The Queen!" He coughed, glanced at Tom, then looked away. "Mr Bull should be in any time now," he said.

"Mr Bull?"

"The hangman." Grimly smiled. "I'm sure he'll be delighted to meet up with you! Delighted, I'm absolutely sure."

The cart was old and piled high with loaves. As it rolled into Whitehall Palace a couple of guards wandered over and glanced at the driver, a small, plump man who was also completely white – being covered from head to toe in flour.

"You're late!" one of the guards said.

"The oven went out," the driver – who was also the baker – replied. "The fool of a boy fell asleep in the night." The second guard was meanwhile searching underneath the cart. "What's going on?" the driver exclaimed. "You know me well enough. What do you think I'm hiding?"

"We had some trouble here last night," the first guard explained. His partner straightened up. "All right! Move on..."

The cart continued round to the kitchen entrance. The driver looked left and right, then whistled softly. A moment later, all the loaves heaved and separated as two figures, now as flour-covered as the driver, pulled themselves from under the pile.

"Thanks, Walter," Moll said.

"You owe me one for this, Moll," the baker muttered. He took a tray off the back.

161

"Give me one minute."

Moll Cutpurse and Gamaliel Ratsey looked a bizarre sight as they crept over to the kitchen of Whitehall Palace; a girl in boy's clothes and a man in a mask, both of them bristling with weapons and covered in flour. Ratsey's mask was a small one and suited his name for it was in the shape of a rat. Moll had tried to stop him from wearing it but Ratsey had insisted. It was either with the mask or not at all.

The kitchen was heaving with cooks, undercooks, waiters and boys already hard at work on the midday meal. Half a deer was rotating slowly on a metal spit turned by a fat boy who was sweating as much as the meat he was cooking. Ratsey and Moll waited at the door as the baker went past them, calling out "Fresh bread!" He walked to the far side of the kitchen. Just as he reached the counter, the tray tipped and the rolls went everywhere. The baker cried out and crashed to the ground. At that moment, with all eyes on the accident, Moll and Ratsey slipped through the kitchen and out the other side.

They found themselves in a larder, filled with cured hams, salted fish and pickled vegetables. For a moment Moll thought they had walked into a cupboard but there was a second door leading out and, taking it, they found themselves in a long passage.

"Which way?" Ratsey whispered.

"Up!"

They reached a staircase and hurried up. A second corridor led directly above the first, but this one was much more smartly decorated with tapestries, curving wooden tables and oil paintings.

"We've got to find the Presence Chamber," Ratsey said.

"Will the Queen be there?"

"She might be. If she's not there, we can try the Watching Chamber and if she's not there she might be in the Great Hall."

"If she's not there, we're in trouble," Moll said.

And that was when the Gentlemen Pensioners appeared. Not just two or three but an entire platoon on a routine patrol. They had stepped out of an archway at the end of the corridor and now they were gazing at Moll and Ratsey with a mixture of astonishment and outrage.

"What was that about trouble?" Ratsey said.

"Back!" Moll shouted.

They turned and ran the way they came, aware of the thunder of feet and the clatter of weapons behind them.

"In here!" Ratsey had reached another door and, grabbing hold of Moll, dragged her in.

They found themselves in a library, a room filled from floor to ceiling with precious books, many of them bound in gold and silver, some of them also decorated with pearls and precious stones. Two windows looked out on to gardens and a tennis court but there was no way to climb down. The room had only one door and even as Ratsey slid a heavy chair across to block it, they heard the sound of the guards and the hammering of fists on wood. There was no way out. They were trapped.

Ratsey threw himself into the chair, adding his weight to the barrier while Moll checked the windows, quickly returning with a shake of her head. Outside, the hammering stopped. The guards knew where they were. All they had to do now was wait.

"Well, so much for that," Ratsey muttered. It was impossible to see his face behind the rat mask but he sounded only a little bit depressed. "It looks like we're stuck."

"Maybe we can explain..." Moll began.

"I wonder if we'll be hanged, drawn and quartered?" Ratsey mused. "I always wondered what it would be like..."

Outside the door, the hammering started again but this time with some solid metal tool. A panel of wood splintered. An axe-head jutted through. Ratsey drew his sword. Moll drew hers. And then one of the bookshelves swung open and a man stepped into the room.

He was an old man, dressed in a black robe, with a beard reaching down to his chest.

Curiously, he was smiling. Even more curiously, he was holding a cat.

"Moll Cutpurse and Gamaliel Ratsey, I believe," he said. He spoke with a Welsh accent. "You'd better come this way. The guards will be breaking in any minute."

A second axe slammed into the door. Another panel of wood cracked open.

"Who are you?" Moll demanded.

"And where did you come from?" Ratsey asked.

"I'm not sure we have time for introductions," the old man said.

The door was struck twice more. One of its hinges shattered. Now they could hear the guards, shouting in triumph.

"This way!" The old man gestured at the secret passage behind the bookshelf. Moll and Ratsey exchanged a glance, then ran in. The old man and the cat followed them. The shelf of books swung shut behind them.

"Follow me," the old man said.

They were in a narrow passage lined with bricks on both sides and lit by a series of oil lamps. It seemed to run the entire length of the palace with other passages and even staircases leading off. It was almost like a secret palace within the palace, a hidden network connecting every room in the building. The old man knew exactly where they were going. Humming softly to himself, and still carrying the

165

cat, he hurried on ahead, not even pausing to check that the other two were behind. At last he stopped beside a large panel of wood.

"This will lead you into the Presence Chamber," he said. "I can't promise that the Queen will be there. You may have scared her away with all the fuss. But you may still find what you want."

"Who are you?" Moll asked.

"My name is John Dee."

Ratsey was suspicious. "How did you know who we were? And why are you helping us?"

"Either we can spend all day talking or you can go in there and save the boy," Dee replied. He paused for a reply but there was none. "I'll wish you a good day," he said.

"Good luck!"

Dr Dee turned and walked away from Moll and Ratsey, heading back down the passage. For a moment neither of them spoke. Either they were going mad or the last words had just been spoken by the cat.

At length, Moll laid a hand on the wooden panel and turned to Ratsey. "Are you ready?" she whispered.

"Yes."

"Then let's go."

She pushed.

The Presence Chamber was full that morning: Privy Councillors and Clerks, Gentlemen Ushers and Grooms, Bishops and Ambassadors. But even as Moll stumbled through a curtain and into the centre of the darkly panelled room, she realized that she had failed. The throne was empty. There was no Queen.

For a moment, everyone froze. To the assembled courtiers it was as if two nightmare creatures – one with the face of a rat – had suddenly been conjured out of thin air. As Moll and Ratsey stood there, taking everything in, the spell was suddenly broken. Swords and knives were drawn. Doors crashed open and soldiers appeared, running and shouting. Ratsey had a knife in one hand and a sword in another. Moll also held a dagger. But it was useless. They were completely surrounded. And they were outnumbered by at least fifty to one.

"Put down your weapons!" someone exclaimed.

"This is the Queen's Presence Chamber!"

"Traitors!"

Ratsey twisted round, his knife raised. "I'm not a traitor!" he said.

"We came to see the Queen!" Moll cried, knowing it was useless. The guards were already moving in. She and Ratsey could kill one, two, three of them. But it wouldn't do any good. They would be cut down where they stood.

"Where did you come from?" A man who looked as if he was in charge had forced his way to the front of the circle. It was the man with green eyes who had spoken to Tom only the night before. "What do you want with Her Majesty?"

"To tell her she was wrong about Tom!"

"Who?"

"The boy! The boy who attacked her!"

"You know him? You're part of his company?"

"Yes – we know him. No – we're not with him."

The man with green eyes became alert, his face suddenly grave. "Take them!" he snapped.

Before Ratsey and Moll could do anything, they were seized from behind. Their arms were wrenched back, their weapons falling uselessly to the ground. Ratsey's mask was torn off along with Moll's hat. In seconds, they were completely pinned down, unable to move.

"You're making a mistake!" Moll shouted. "You've got this all wrong."

"Take them to prison for interrogation," the man with the green eyes said. "And I want to know how they got in here!"

"Yes, Lord Moorfield." One of the guards bowed and signalled with his head. Moll and Ratsey were pulled backwards out of the room.

They had almost reached the door before Moll's brain began to buzz.

Sir William Hawkins. His last cry: "Go to

Moorfield." *Not a place! A person!*

"Moorfield!" she cried out. "Tom is the boy you're looking for. The boy from Framlingham! He's the boy you sent Hawkins to find!"

But Moll was already out of the room.

The heavy door slammed shut as she and Ratsey were dragged away.

They knew when a hanging was going to take place. Just after eleven a hush descended on Newgate. The shouting of the prisoners, the mad laughter, the booming of doors and the rattling of chains suddenly stopped and the corridors seemed empty, haunted. Then there was a groan as one door opened. And everyone knew. They had come for Tom Falconer.

Tom stood up as the door crashed open and Mr Bull, the hangman, came in. He glanced first at James Grimly, who was cowering on the bunk with his head in his hands, then at Tom. "Good morning," he said. "I believe you and I have an appointment."

Tom nodded. The hangman wasn't at all what he had expected. Mr Bull was a small, neat man dressed in a blue, velvet tunic. Now he gestured with one hand and four guards marched in to surround Tom. "This won't take a minute," he said.

One of the guards grabbed Tom's arms and, ignoring his wound, tied his hands behind his back. Then, with Mr Bull at the front, and the guards on all four sides, Tom was led down a corridor, past a series of barred doors. The corridor was arched, the brickwork ancient and blood red. The straw under his feet was filthy but Tom couldn't smell it. He couldn't hear anything. All his senses seemed to be failing him ... even his sight. The darkness seemed to be rushing in.

They walked to the end of the corridor and down a staircase carved out of stone. Tom had thought they would be going outside the prison but the stairs led to another corridor and then to a final archway. The scaffold stood in a room at the far end.

The strange thing was, Tom wasn't afraid. He was amazed. The scaffold was just how he had always imagined it. It was exactly the same as the drawings he had seen schoolboys make in Framlingham: three pieces of wood, a trapdoor with a lever and, hanging over it, a noose. As simple as that.

The scaffold had been erected in a great chamber, closed to the outside world apart from a series of small windows set too high up to see through. The chamber was shaped like the dome of a cathedral, the walls made of bare brick. The size of the place made the scaffold seem small and insignificant.

Mr Bull coughed discreetly and the party moved forward. Nine steps – Tom would count them now. He reached the first and stumbled. With his hands tied behind him and unable to balance himself, he might have fallen but one of the guards reached out and steadied him. He began to climb.

As he took the first step, a figure appeared from underneath the scaffold. This was a huge man, bare-chested, with a black hood over his face. Tom glanced enquiringly at Mr Bull who shook his head. Tom understood. Mr Bull organized the business. He was, if you like, the artist. But the actual work itself, that had to be left to a hired hand.

Tom reached the top of the scaffold and stood in the middle of the platform. He could just make out the cracks of the trapdoor that would open when the lever was pulled. The wooden planks creaked slightly underneath him. He tried to swallow but his mouth was too dry. The hooded man had followed him up and leaned forward to pull the noose around his head. For a moment his arms, and the huge muscles of his chest, were close to Tom's face. Tom caught the slightly bitter smell of the man's sweat. He jerked away and felt the touch of the rope around his neck. It was hairy and tickled.

Tom hadn't seen any drummers, but suddenly the chamber was filled with a steady drumming, starting low but rising in volume as the beat got faster. He had expected a blindfold but none had been offered. What should he look at? What would be the last thing he ever saw? He tried to concentrate his sight on the daylight streaming in through the upper windows but out of the corner of his eye he could see the hooded man reach for the lever.

Tom closed his eyes.

Mr Bull nodded. The hooded man's hand tightened.

"Stop!"

It was a woman's voice, loud and authoritative, the sort of voice that had to be obeyed. The single word had come from the door but it seemed to explode in the chamber, echoing off the walls. The drumming stopped instantly. The hooded man, Mr Bull and the four guards fell to their knees. Tom slowly turned his head, the noose rubbing against his neck.

Queen Elizabeth swept into the room and she had never looked more awesome or more majestic. She was wearing a billowing dress of black satin decorated with gold buckles rising all the way up the front to her neck. Her face was surrounded by a collar of dazzling white with a great band of white pearls hanging from her neck. She had come to a halt in a circle of light lancing down from one of the windows and in the dark interior she seemed to burn gold and white and every colour of the spectrum. Her eyes burned brightest of all. And they were staring at Tom.

"Bring the boy down," she said.

For a moment nobody moved. Then everyone ran for the steps, fighting to be the first to reach the boy who was now dangling from the rope, having fainted where he stood.

FIVE HEADS

The Queen came to see Tom a few days later.

He had been taken to the Tower, not to one of the prisons but to a comfortable room overlooking the Thames. As soon as he had been strong enough to walk, he had tried the door and had been pleased to discover that it wasn't locked. There had been other surprises. The room had a bed with sheets of pure linen. And Tom had been brought clothes that were finer and more expensive than anything he had ever seen. He had been given wonderful food. The wine had come in a real glass.

And now, here was the Queen of England, standing in his room. Just the two of them. Alone. Impossible!

Tom bowed low, fixing his eyes on the floor. He heard the Queen sweep into the room and sit down on a chair. After a long silence, wondering if he dared, Tom looked up.

"They call you Tom Falconer," the Queen said.

"Yes, Your Majesty."

"Tom…" The Queen was staring at him with a whole range of contrary emotions in her eyes. She seemed happy and sad, angry and pleased, aloof but uncertain, royal and yet somehow afraid. It was late in the afternoon. The sun was beginning to set. The Thames was flowing from silver to a burning red. "Sit down, Tom," the Queen said.

There was only one chair in the room. Tom sat down on the bed.

"How is your wound, child?"

"Much better, thank you, Your Majesty." His wound had been cleaned and bandaged. It was hurting now – a sure sign that it was beginning to heal.

The Queen bowed her head.

"I have done you great wrong," she said.

"It's all right, Your Majesty. You weren't to know…"

The Queen waved a hand to silence him and fell silent. Sitting on the chair, just a few centimetres away, she looked much more like the old woman she undoubtedly was. Her skin was heavily made-up, but Tom could still see the wrinkles. He already knew (although it shamed him to remember) that her bright red hair was a wig. Her teeth were entirely black. And yet her pale skin and bright blue eyes reminded him of someone. He wondered who.

"I have to talk to you about … other matters, Tom," the Queen said. "But I shall begin with Dr Mobius and the Garden Players." She paused. "As I am sure you've guessed, they weren't an acting company at all. In fact they were Spanish, members of a secret organization called the *Garduna*. They were going to kill me, even though they knew they would all die themselves. And they would have succeeded, if it hadn't been for you."

She smiled.

"As you probably know, the man who calls himself Dr Mobius had bribed one of my officers. Sir Richard Brooke…"

"The man with the scar!"

"A man who will have more than a scar by the time I've finished with him! He worked for my Lord Chamberlain. Between them, they choose which plays I see. Sir Richard was paid well to introduce the Garden Players. But soon it's going to be his turn to pay…"

"How did you find out, Your Majesty?" Tom asked. He was slowly getting used to the fact that he was having a quiet chat with the richest and most powerful woman in the world. He was even beginning to enjoy it. "How did you find out that I wasn't on their side?"

"You have your two friends to thank for that."

"Two…?"

"Moll Cutpurse and Gamaliel Ratsey."

"What?" Ratsey had *helped* him? The very thought made Tom's head spin.

"They broke into my Presence Chamber and although I had already retired, they had the good fortune to come upon one of my spies. A man by the name of Henry Moorfield."

"Moorfield?" Tom gasped. "I thought it was a place!"

"You were told to go to Moorfield by Sir William Hawkins. I know. And this is where it gets difficult, Tom. This is where it finishes and where it starts."

To Tom's astonishment, the Queen rose from the chair, came over and sat down next to him on the bed. Gently, she laid her hands on his face, one underneath his chin and one on the side of his cheek and turned him so that she could look into his eyes. At the same time, Tom looked into her eyes – he couldn't avoid it – and saw how sad they had become.

"Listen to me," she said, and her voice was a whisper. "You must never tell anyone else what I am going to tell you. Believe me, Tom. It's a secret that could destroy us both – and the entire country with us."

She hesitated. Then… "More than forty years ago, when I was just sixteen years old, I made a dreadful mistake. My father had died and the king – Edward – was only a boy,

177

younger than you.

"He was too young to reign on his own, so the Council elected a man to look after him – a Protector. That man was called Edward Seymour. And the mistake I made was to fall in love with his brother.

"Thomas Seymour – yes, he had the same name as you – was a rogue and a ruffian and a fool. But he was also handsome, brave, and he made me laugh. He was much older than me and he was married but … well, one thing led to another and he…" She found it difficult to frame the words. "He left me with a child!

"Those were dangerous times, Tom. The day I learned I was pregnant, Thomas Seymour was arrested – for treason." She sighed. "He was no more a traitor than I was but, as I told you, he was a fool, and two months later, he lost his head. And there was I, left behind, carrying his baby! If anyone had found out, Tom, believe me, my head would have gone too. As it was, I was sent here, to the Tower and interrogated. Luckily, I kept my head. And my secret. But it was close.

"I left the Tower and went to Hatfield and it was there, in complete secrecy, that I gave birth to a child, a boy. I called him Thomas, after his father, but I saw him for only one day. It was too dangerous to keep him close. It hurt me, Tom, but I knew I had no choice. A servant of mine had the baby passed to a wet-nurse and smuggled away. He was taken to a family in Suffolk who agreed to adopt him. They also changed his name. They called him Robert."

Tom stared. He couldn't believe what he was hearing. And he was already beginning to see what was about to come.

"After I lost the child, I thought about him every hour of every day," the Queen went on. "But then a time came when I had to force myself to forget him, to pretend that he didn't exist." She sighed. "It was difficult becoming queen. It was difficult staying queen. And it's *still* murderously difficult being queen. And admitting to having an illegitimate child by a man executed for treason forty-four years ago would only make it all the more difficult. I've had no choice. I've had to forget my own child."

"What happened to him?" Tom asked. But he already knew.

"Something went wrong. The family that was supposed to be looking after him failed me. Thomas – or Robert as he now was – grew up to become the falcon keeper at Framlingham Castle. But then there was an accident. He fell off a horse…"

"You're talking about my father," Tom said.

"Yes."

There was a long silence.

"You're my grandmother," Tom said.

"Yes." The Queen took Tom's hand in her own, holding it as if it were a precious object rather than flesh and blood. "I never knew your father had died. And I never knew that you had been born," she said. "Not until recently."

"And so you sent Sir William Hawkins to find me?"

"Yes. He didn't know who you really were, although he may have guessed. He was a spy. He was clever."

"You know how he died?"

"Yes. We managed to get the truth out of that scoundrel, Ratsey, and believe me, Tom, he should lose his head for his part in all this. But, well, we can discuss that later."

The Queen stood up. "I'll come back this evening," she said. "Then we can talk again."

"Wait a minute!" It suddenly occurred to Tom that he had completely dropped the "Your Majesties". And he had just told the Queen what to do! "There is one thing," he said. "You told me that nobody must know. So what you're saying is, I'm your grandson. But I'm not going to be king."

"The question of who'll be king is something the whole country has been asking," the Queen replied. "And I wish Parliament would stop bothering me about it. I could introduce you, if you wanted, Tom. And perhaps the people might accept you. On the other hand, it could lead to a bloody civil war." She shrugged. "Do you want to be king?"

"I don't think so," Tom said.

"Well, I can see you've inherited a little common sense," the Queen said. She paused, suddenly serious. "But think about this, Tom. I can help you become whatever you want. Think about it. We'll meet again this evening."

That evening, Tom and the Queen met for the last time.

"I want to ask you a favour," Tom said.

"Go on."

"I've been thinking about Florian. He was one of the Garden Players. Have you…?" Tom hesitated to say it.

"He hasn't been executed, Tom. Not yet."

"Will you spare him, Your Majesty?" Tom blushed without quite knowing why. "I know he was part of it, but I don't think he wanted to be. Dr Mobius was his uncle. He just did what he was told. The same as me when I was at the Pig's Head."

The Queen didn't look pleased. "It's not a good idea to spare your enemies," she said, "because it gives all your other enemies ideas." She softened. "But if you really think he was forced into it, I could just have him tortured…"

"Couldn't you just let him go?"

"If you insist. Is there anything else?"

Tom smiled. "I was wondering about Moll and Ratsey…"

"Two vagabonds! A pickpocket and a highwayman. I have to say, Tom, for someone with royal blood in you, you've been keeping some pretty low company. But you're alive and I have them to thank for it. What do you want me to do with them? Don't tell me you want me to knight them!"

"Will you let them go?"

"I already have. Mistress Cutpurse left with a bag of gold for her pains."

"What about Ratsey?"

"He was lucky to escape with his life." Suddenly the Queen was stern. "Maybe he wasn't entirely to blame for what he became, Tom. And every man deserves a second chance. But I tell you this. If he ever ends up on one of my scaffolds – and I'm certain he will – I won't be there to help."

"I understand."

The Queen sat next to Tom once again and held him in her arms. "But what of you, Tom? Have you thought what you're going to do? I can give you a house and land. I can make you a lord…"

"I don't want to be a lord, Your Majesty." Tom smiled. "I want to be an actor!"

"What?"

"There's a man I met. His name is William Shakespeare…"

The Queen nodded. "Yes. I've heard of him. I'm told he's rather good."

"I met him when I was trying to get into the Rose Theatre. We got on quite well and I'm sure he'd help me if..."

"I'm not sure I approve of players," the Queen said. "They're a rowdy lot at the best of times. But if you're sure that's what you really want..."

"It is. More than anything in the world."

"I'll have a word with Master Shakespeare." She stood up and once again she was sad. "I think it would be easier for both of us if we kept apart," she said. "But if you ever need my help, Tom, I'm very easy to find."

"I'm sure, Your Majesty."

"And if you can't be my grandson, you can still be my friend. After all, you did save my life."

"I'll always be your servant." Tom bowed.

The Queen turned and left the room.

A few weeks later, rehearsals began for a new play that was to be performed at the Rose Theatre in the early spring. The play was called *Romeo and Juliet*. It was a love story.

Tom had only a small part in the play. He had been cast as a servant and he had only a few lines. But it was a start. And what mattered to him was that he was an actor, an official member of the Company of the Admiral's Men.

He had seen Moll only once since winter had ended. She had come to the theatre to wish him luck and had stayed just long enough to pick-pocket a couple of spectators before heading off to a thieves' dinner-and-dance in Shoreditch. Gamaliel Ratsey had gone straight back to Suffolk without bothering to say goodbye. Tom had to admit he was rather glad. The trouble with Ratsey was you never knew if he was going to shake your hand or cut your throat.

"Tom!" Shakespeare was calling him now, a great pile of papers in one hand, a feather quill in the other. The two of them spent much of their time together. Tom loved giving Shakespeare ideas for new plays. In return, Shakespeare was teaching Tom how to read.

Tom hurried to join his friend.

At the same time, a short way up the Thames, four men and one woman were gazing in Tom's direction, as if trying to see what he was doing. Dr Mobius was the first of them. Then came James Grimly, Sir Richard Brooke and finally Sebastian and Henrietta Slope. They were almost unrecognizable by now, as they'd been there for several weeks. Five heads on five spikes high above London Bridge.

Beneath them, the river flowed gently past, the water glistening in the dying light.

Goodnight, goodnight!
Parting is such sweet sorrow
That I shall say goodnight
till it be morrow...

AFTERWORD

This is the chapter you don't have to read.

But for those of you who want to know, a lot of *The Devil and his Boy* is based on truth. Many of the characters, for example, were alive in 1593. Elizabeth I and Shakespeare, of course, but also Gamaliel Ratsey, Moll Cutpurse, Philip Henslowe, Lord Strange, Edmund Tilney (Master of the Revels), Dr John Dee and even Mr Bull, the hangman.

I have tried to describe London as it was in the sixteenth century. Paul's Walk really was at the heart of the City – it was the place where people went to find work – and there was an open area called Moorfield, just north of Moorgate. The Rose Theatre, Newgate Prison and Whitehall were all much as I've described and the Banqueting Hall at Whitehall really was made of cloth (it was replaced with a solid structure in the reign of King James).

186

Framlingham is also a real town. You can still visit the castle with its peculiar twisted chimneys. Even now, nobody knows why they were built.

As to the events described in this book... It is certainly true that the young Elizabeth had a close relationship with Thomas Seymour, brother of the Protector. It was also rumoured that she carried his child. Elizabeth herself wrote, "...that there goeth rumours abroad which be greatly both against my honour and honesty (which above all things I esteem) which be these: that I am in the Tower and with child by my lord Admiral..."

There were also many people who hated the Queen and wanted her dead – mainly the Spanish. The *Garduna* was a secret organization, closely linked with the Inquisition. Its members were also known as the Holy Warriors of Spain.

Moll Cutpurse was a famous thief of the sixteenth century. She is even the subject of a play – *The Roaring Girl*. Moll did dress up in boys' clothes. She was involved with a "school for crime". And she was the daughter of a shoemaker. It's nice to know that she lived until she was seventy, a remarkable age, before she died of dropsy.

Gamaliel Ratsey was less fortunate. The most famous highwayman of his time, Ratsey did have noble parents and had served in Ireland before he took to crime (many thieves were unemployed soldiers). He was also well-known for his horrible masks. Eight years after this book ends, Ratsey was betrayed by a friend and taken prisoner. He was hanged.

John Dee is an interesting character. He was Queen Elizabeth's personal magician, a Welshman who spent much of his life searching for the secret of how to turn base metal into gold. Dee also owned a "stone of vision" – I didn't make it up. There's no record, however, of his owning a talking cat!

Wherever possible, in *The Devil and his Boy*, I have tried to use accurate details from the sixteenth century. For example, dinner at the Pig's Head would have cost you "sixpence downstairs and eightpence up". London boys did enjoy throwing mud balls at strangers. And so on.

That said, however, it is quite possible that teachers will find some mistakes in this book. These mistakes are entirely deliberate. I put them in to keep the teachers happy.

ANTHONY HOROWITZ

GROOSHAM GRANGE
Anthony Horowitz

New pupils are made to sign their names in blood...

The assistant headmaster has no reflection...

The French teacher disappears whenever there's a full moon...

Groosham Grange, David Eliot's new school, is a very weird place indeed!

"One of the funniest books of the year."
Young Telegraph

"Hilarious ... speeds along at full tilt from page to page."
Books for Keeps